For my Mother

who taught me you're never too old
to believe in yourself again

What others are saying about Mark Miller's writing...

"...the best one in the series...a fascinating tale...well written and very entertaining. There were numerous twists and turns in the story that kept me guessing all the way until the end of the book.

This story was clearly well thought out and flowed very well, even while dealing with a girl who found herself skipping randomly back and forth through time. While that could have made it difficult to follow, it was well enough written that I had no problems keeping track of whether Nyssa was in the past, present, or future of Empyrean. And though I won't spoil it for you, I absolutely loved the ending.

I would recommend this book to anyone who enjoys intricately designed fantasy worlds containing a rich history that clearly shines throughout the story."

-Molly White, Mom Kat Reads

"Miller has a lot of whatever it is that makes a good fantasy writer...Whatever the secret is to writing great fantasy, The Secret Queen is the result."

-Reader's Favorite Book Reviews

"There is a musical quality to the way Miller writes that makes the reader want to pick up more of his books. Something else that should be considered is that these books have very strong female protagonists, none of the wimpy ones we see too often nowadays, so it's a great choice for teen girls."

-Midwest Book Reviews

Books by
Mark Miller

The Empyrical Tales
   Book I: Journey of the Fourth Queen
   Book II: Search for the Lost Queen
   Book III: Mystery of the Secret Queen
   Book IV: History of the First Queen

Small World Global Protection Agency
   #001 New Kids on the Rock
   #002 Bulls and Burglars
   #003 The Not So Perfect Game

Promise of Tomorrow

Dinosaur George and the Paleonauts
   Episode One: Raptor Island

HISTORY OF THE FIRST QUEEN

Mark Miller

MillerWords, LLC

MillerWords, LLC
PO Box 861074
Shawnee, KS 66286

First Edition

For discounts on bulk purchases, please contact MillerWords Educational Sales at **Sales@MillerWords.com**

Printed in the United States of America

2 4 6 8 10 9 7 5 3 1

Library of Congress Control Number: 2019915151

ISBN: 978-0-9996195-9-9

Chapter 1

The First Memory

A girl, running.

She could not stop running.

Nyssa did not know why, but her feet kept moving on their own.

For a moment, she thought maybe she knew why. Something to do with home, except she did not have a home.

Not anymore.

Something massive collapsed in front of her. She could not slow down. Nyssa quickly dodged the thing, whatever it was.

From the glimpses between frequent periods of squeezing her eyes shut, this place did not look familiar. No sidewalks. No houses. She heard noise though.

Terrible noise.

The noise almost drowned out the music in her head. Almost. Things seemed to be crashing all around her. Not the sudden shattering like when she dropped a plate. Nyssa always seemed to drop a plate when it was her turn to do the dishes. This sound had more to it.

Nyssa opened her eyes again. Something that looked like a leg passed in front of her. She thought it could not be possible because it was longer than her whole body. Nyssa considered herself petite, not small. Still, she had never seen anyone with legs taller than her head. An instant later, the second leg passed in front of her. Somewhere up above, the enormous body blocked the blinding sunlight.

When the figure kept moving, Nyssa slammed her eyes shut to protect her from the bright light. For some reason, she thought it should have been darker.

Then a memory came back to her. She *knew* it was supposed to be darker. Under the roar of this chaos, she *knew* it was supposed to be quiet. Her mind slipped back to only a minute before now, but it strangely felt like ages ago.

Nyssa could remember the music in her head. She always had music in her head, but she did not have much else. She could remember a peculiar place. The room looked familiar, but also entirely new to her. She tried to remember the room. But it was not simply a room.

A shop.

Some kind of shop, Nyssa recalled. She did not remember how she got there or when. All she could remember was this long, dark shop. *That's right*, she thought, *it was dark*. She remembered how odd it seemed that the room was lit only by a squatty candle. The light barely reflected off the dusty glass top of the display case that held it. Some of the wax overflowed the candle holder and streaked down the front of the display case before it cooled enough to stop moving.

The only other light came from the front of the shop. The tall windows had been poorly newspapered over and some areas showed where dried soap had been smeared to keep outsiders from peering into the gloom. Most of the faded paper drooped to the floor thanks to years old dry tape. This allowed sunlight to creep in to about the front quarter of the showroom.

At least, Nyssa thought of it as a showroom. The apparently abandoned shop held all sorts of things for show. Many of the items had an otherworldly feel to them. Nyssa had never seen objects like these for sale at TG&Y. In fact, she had never seen a shop like this anywhere.

Nyssa could not specifically remember any of the products. She thought they seemed to be handmade out of things pulled from a dumpster right before the trash truck came to haul them off.

Except, she did remember one thing. It stood out, white and polished. Everything else in the shop seemed to have been surrendered to time for who knew how long. This huge skull had been cared for, dusted occasionally.

Her last foster brother, not from her current family, could have told her what kind of dinosaur it was. He loved dinosaurs. Nyssa could tell from his countless books that it was a dinosaur skull. She guessed maybe a spino-something. That was only a guess. The frightening jaw held teeth as long as her arm. The mouth looked long enough to swallow her in one bite.

Something strange caught Nyssa's eye. This skull looked unnatural. The back edge looked flat, as if the head had been sliced off the body, maybe by a laser or something.

That terrible noise yanked Nyssa from her memory. She thought maybe she was in that shop a minute ago, but not now. That shop was in her world.

This was not *her* world.

The sound did not sound like a car crash or a jet engine. It did sound angry. She knew without opening her eyes that someone was fighting. With as many foster homes as she had lived in, not in the good ones, she knew too well what fighting sounded like. However, this fight sounded like buildings being toppled. Some huge demolition crew smashed everything around her.

Nyssa tried to open her eyes again. Looking down, it surprised her to see her feet still moving, splashing in water. She had not stopped running. Luckily for her, she kept moving. Whoever was fighting towered over her and did not seem to notice she was there.

The bright sun still hurt her eyes after the darkness of the shop, but she could start to see things now. Nyssa decided keeping her head down would be the safest option, so mostly she saw trampled grass along the edge of a small river. Occasionally, a gigantic foot filled her vision and Nyssa would change direction seconds before being crushed or splashed.

It did not seem to matter which way she went, the fight surrounded her. And that noise engulfed her.

The noise reminded her of school in a way. There always seemed to be a hum. Someone always had something to say, usually about her. Nyssa lost her parents before she could even remember their faces. She had wonderful foster parents for a long time. Then something happened. He lost his job or something like that. Nyssa could not quite remember.

Then her life really went bad. Three foster families and three schools later, Nyssa found herself in a new high school with no friends. Over the past four years, she barely stayed in one place long enough to make any friends. It became easier for Nyssa to close herself off from the possibility, while listening to her music. She decided she did not want any friends. She wanted to be left alone. She liked her music and it kept her company.

Either because of her solitude, or that high school kids are still only kids, Nyssa always heard that hum. In the cafeteria, or gym, or classroom, someone always had something to say about her. The whispered words usually ended with a hushed laugh, or worse, a frown.

Nyssa liked to be alone, but she did not like feeling lonely. She listened to all kinds of music and even wrote her own songs. That sometimes took away the loneliness.

Right now, she did not feel lonely at all. When she looked up, Nyssa could see giants all around her. Giant men collided into each other relentlessly.

The battle circled her like an endless chaotic dance. Nyssa had only been at their feet for a moment, but she felt like they had been fighting for days, maybe years.

As they moved, the warriors unintentionally forced her path toward the center of their chaos, waist deep into the river. Finally, Nyssa had nowhere else to go. A huge stone blocked her path and water glided by her. Nyssa stared at the rock, she stared into it. It looked like no stone she had seen before. Small, silver speckles sparkled on its polished surface.

And that terrible noise seemed to come from inside of it.

Nyssa feared if she stared too long at its blackness, the stone might somehow pull her in. Instead, she decided to put her back to the rock. From there, she could see the battle around her.

It seemed the cataclysmic events around her were only being caused by a handful of men. Nyssa counted eight in total, if they could all be called men. Their fight raged on a wide open plain, but continually spiraled around this mysterious rock in the middle of a lonely river.

It seemed to be four versus four.

The size of each giant made Nyssa feel like a baby instead of a sixteen year old girl. Two of them looked more like men with their long beards and solid muscles. One must have been older with his white hair, while the other had dark brown hair and darker skin. Nyssa guessed them to be on the same team. Their third teammate almost looked human except he had the head of a bird on his bronze shoulders. He reminded Nyssa of a character from a mummy movie.

While their fourth ally looked strange, he was not the strangest. His body somewhat resembled a human, but he had the neck and tail of a dinosaur. He snapped his tail with dangerous precision. When he extended his neck, he towered over his foes.

Nyssa thought of these four being on the same team because the other four giants looked identical. It almost made her sick to look at them.

These four looked like monsters. Slime dripped off of them and smoke seeped out of their blackened pores. Each creature had three eyes, always looking in different directions. Nyssa thought they could probably see the whole battlefield all at once. They were covered with strange symbols that looked carved into their skin.

The girl watched these giants battle from her spot in the shadow of the black rock, cool water soaking her lower half. Instinctively, she began to cheer for the more human of the fighters.

Yet neither side seemed to gain an advantage. They traded blows, but none would fall. Nyssa studied the old man with the white beard. Even with his green robes shredded, he reminded her of someone. She thought maybe he looked like Santa

Claus, but he was not nearly fat enough. The one with dark hair could have been his brother. Although he looked younger than the white-bearded giant, the look in his eyes made him seem older to Nyssa.

While she watched, Nyssa felt something slipping around her, wrapping her up. She looked down to see nothing and realized the feeling was in her head, but it came from the unusual black stone. The flakes of silver sparkled at her like an invitation to come inside, if a stone could have an *inside*. Nyssa did not want to know what might be in there. She could hear and feel that terrible sound and it scared her.

Nyssa squeezed her eyes shut again. She tried to remember the lyrics to a song, any song.

She remembered walking home from school. Nyssa did not like calling it *home*. She had not had a real home for a long time. They did give her food and a place to sleep. When they fought, they usually did not yell at her, only each other.

Today, the walk to their house seemed different. Today, more people crowded the street. Then Nyssa saw a police car, lights flashing. Behind the car, a red and yellow fire truck blocked the view of her foster parents' house.

Nyssa ran the rest of the way, pushing through the crowd. She spotted her younger foster sister on the sidewalk next to her foster dad. They did not see her because they were staring at the smoldering remains of their house.

Then Nyssa's foster mother charged at her from the muddy lawn. Fire hoses still sprayed the charred wood creating a rainbow from the afternoon sun behind the furious woman.

"This is your fault," she screamed.

It's always my fault, thought Nyssa.

The haggard woman continued, "You caused this!"

"What happened?" asked Nyssa, aware of the obvious house fire.

"You left the stove on when you cooked breakfast this morning," screamed her foster mother.

"But I had cereal," Nyssa tried to explain.

"Liar," shouted the woman. Then she lunged at Nyssa. A nearby paramedic stopped her from hitting the defenseless girl.

Nyssa took a few steps back.

"I wish you were never born," said the foster mother, still clawing at her.

Nyssa turned and ran.

Always running.

But she did not cry. Nyssa knew she did not cause the fire. She knew she had to stay away until child services came for her.

She kept running.

She ran until she found herself in a new world populated with warring giants.

Something came before that though, thought Nyssa.

Then that terrible noise stopped.

This caused the giants to instantly stop fighting. All eight of them turned to look at her. Except they were not looking at her, they were looking at the black stone with the hypnotic silver speckles.

Suddenly that terrible sound came back louder than before. To Nyssa, it sounded like a thousand plates shattering at the center of a thousand car wrecks, except that it did not. It could not sound like that because it also sounded wet and sticky. The sound went from her ears to her brain and poked like little needles. It pushed any thoughts of music out of her head.

The shiny black rock cracked. Then it split apart into four equal pieces. Something moved at the center. The river bubbled around the rock. Nyssa could feel the water getting warmer and she climbed onto dry ground.

"Parasauratitan, now!" shouted the white-bearded man.

The dinosaur-like creature nodded at the end of his long neck and threw something to the man closest to the vibrating black stone. "Horus, the Atumval," called the Parasauratitan with his resonating voice.

Horus, the birdman, caught the circular object, turned toward the rock and charged. Something inside lashed out so rapidly Nyssa could barely see it. She thought it might have been a tentacle. Whatever it was, it struck Horus. The object in his hand flew away at an unbelievable speed.

Nyssa watched the disc sail away, high into the sky, toward the setting sun.

"All is lost," said the brown-bearded giant. "The Atumval was our only hope of stopping this evil." Then he turned and ran across the plains, in the direction of the lost object.

Nyssa turned her eyes on the ones called Horus and Parasauratitan as they moved to the side of the giant with the white beard. She hastily moved next to them, hopefully safe from whatever was trying to get out of the rock.

The white bearded giant put a large hand in front of Nyssa and nudged her behind him. He said, "This evil has been sealed away for so long, I have forgotten its name."

Then a voice came from inside the broken stone, hidden by noxious fumes. The voice filled the air, but also squirmed inside Nyssa's head, dark and oily. It said, "Don't worry. I remember my name."

More tentacles shot out, knocking the three giants to the ground. A bright flash of light immediately followed and Nyssa covered her head.

The shockwave was the last thing she remembered as the black stone exploded into the air, each of the four pieces flying in four separate directions.

Nyssa felt the pain from the blast. She felt being moved, thrown through the air.

There was something before that though.

Running.

A girl, running.

She ran from her foster parents' smoking home. She did not pay attention to her turns or her time.

When Nyssa finally stopped, she did not recognize the neighborhood. She passed a convenience store, then several stores that had gone out of business. She probably would have liked the record store that used to be in one of the spots, she imagined.

Then a police car turned the corner at the end of the block. Nyssa recognized the driver from the scene of the fire. She did not want to go back to the house before Child Services came. Nyssa did not really like the social worker, but at least she could trust him. Instead of being apprehended, Nyssa ducked into the first open door she could find.

That is where she saw the spino-whatever skull, amid hundreds of other unfinished or broken gadgets and inventions. She ducked behind the counter with the melted candle, hoping the police officer did not see her go in there.

In the back room, she found a man sitting at a cluttered desk. Papers scattered on the floor that looked handwritten in several different languages. Three scrolls, each tied with a red ribbon, lay across the desk. Nyssa guessed the man to be close to forty years old, but his wire frame glasses made him look younger and, in a way, clumsy.

This man stared at a doorway at the back of the room. It seemed to be glowing and Nyssa could not see anything else beyond the door.

"Stay right where you are, miss," said the man, without looking away from the glowing door. "I've been trying to perfect this for twenty years and it may be my last chance to get back."

"Perfect what?" asked Nyssa, finding herself unable to look away from the bright white door, as well.

"I've finally opened a door home," he said. "The bad news is, it's only going to work for one person. Now that you're here, I'm pretty sure it's not going to be me."

Before Nyssa could process the man's words, the little bell above the front door chimed. Someone came into the shop. Nyssa thought it might be the police man, but could not see through the piles of supposed junk. She did not want to wait to find out. She needed an exit now.

The shop owner turned to Nyssa. He pushed his glasses back into place on the bridge of his nose with one ink stained finger.

He said, "I guess I should introduce myself. I'm Karl Lumpkin."

Nyssa divided her attention between Karl and the approaching footsteps. She hesitated for a moment. Her desire for escape became greater than any pleasantries. Without introducing herself, Nyssa ran through the glowing door. The portal instantly closed behind her, leaving Karl in the dark.

He finished his greeting, "Nice to meet you, your majesty."

Chapter 2

The First Story

Castle Empyrean felt different since Olena came back from the Southern Valley. She could not quite tell what it was. Maybe, she thought, she was finally in tune with her magic? Or maybe it was because Isis was really gone?

Both Snow White and Cinderella returned to their homes to make sure they had no new problems. Fury personally carried his queen. William and Aleta stayed in the Southern Valley to oversee the realm until Ovara was ready to take her place there. The Empyrical Wizards stayed hidden. The children seemed to have the rule of the crystal castle.

Olena enjoyed spending time with the new Queen of the Southern Valley. She tried to show Ovara all of the useful magic she could. Ovara seemed to learn fast and even had an easier time with it than Olena.

Olena did not let that disappoint her. If she had learned one thing from her recent travels, it was to have confidence in her own abilities. She knew everything else would happen when it was supposed to.

The peculiar elf Dew Lantisphere returned from the north. She said the last of the elven clans were leaving Empyrean, most going north. Her own family said they would stay because Malika and Marika swore an oath to protect the queens ages ago. They named Dew as their ambassador. She was supposed to relay messages to Castle Empyrean, which meant she could spend more time with Zandria. Olena liked that they each had new friends. Zandria could stay with Dew, while she helped Ovara.

The two young queens enjoyed the opportunity to tell Zandria, Dew and Adam about the amazing things they saw in the south.

This prompted Zandria to want to take the Friesians outside of the castle. She thought they would like drinking from the fresh water of the newly restored Brygos River.

Tihi and Kalis did like the water. It seemed to do them well. After they drank, both Friesians galloped across the grassy plains. They moved at incredible speed and easily galloped out of sight. The horses left the children standing near the canyon edge that surrounded Castle Empyrean. The roar of the Brygos waterfall reminded Olena of the waterfall that hid the Prismata's home back in the east. They spent the better part of the day outside, before everyone returned to the castle for dinner.

In the evening, Kez joined them for their meal. He seemed to like spending time with Sylvan in his Rockhorn body. Of course, Olena realized, Sylvan did not need to eat. Mealtime became one of the only times that the quzzak and the little wooden man were apart. Apparently Sylvan had started learning how to navigate the castle's changing halls. This occupied much of Olena's friends' time.

During their stories, it became apparent that Ovara wanted to avoid the topic of Emperor Li-Am and his Carcharodans. Olena did not mind this. She had one nightmare of him capturing her and Karl Lumpkin again. This made her miss Karl dearly. She wondered where he was and was he safe, if he was still alive.

That night at dinner, the southern tales turned to a new topic. Olena liked to think of it as her secret journey and this part of the secret journey had to do with Horus.

Ovara introduced the man with the hawk's head since she met him first in the Hierakonpolis Market.

"He called himself an immortal," said the Queen of the Southern Valley.

A loud clang interrupted the conversation at the table.

"Ka," shouted Zandria in surprise.

Olena looked around to see Tym, the elven butler, stooping to clean up a spilled tray. He had a look of concern that, Olena guessed, was caused by their talk.

"Forgive me, Your Majesties," said Tym.

"It's okay," said Olena.

"What's wrong with you?" asked Dew.

Tym straightened himself and regained his composure. He said, "Nothing. Only I find it hard to believe you met an Immortal. They don't make themselves easily seen."

"We didn't meet only one," said Ovara.

Olena said, "That's right. We also saw the Para...the Paratis..." she had trouble with his name.

"The Parasauratitan," corrected Kez.

"Right, him too," said Olena.

Tym came to the table and took a seat with the children. Eisenhahn smiled at him from the far end.

"Begging your pardons," Tym began, "My mother told me very little of your journey before she left for the Northern Wood."

"I know Marika was in a hurry to see her sister," said Dew. "I have a feeling those two might be trouble when they're together."

Tym said, "If half the stories are true, you can't imagine how right you are. In all cases, speaking of the Immortals, I am curious how much of the histories the Queen of the Northern Wood shared with you?"

Ovara had not had any history lessons from Snow White, so Olena answered for them both.

She said, "She barely told me anything about the First War for Empyrean. I know the Guardian Hawks found the first queens and they stopped the Forgotten Evil. Then we had a Passing Queen and a Thrice Queen." Olena clicked her tongue against her teeth. "Not too much really."

"Then we should finish this meal and adjourn to more comfortable chambers," said Tym. "There, I will share the story of the First Queen."

Dinner could not end fast enough for Olena. She wanted to hear the story. Apparently, the idea excited everyone else as well. They all skipped dessert, except for Eisenhahn. Dessert always seemed to be his favorite part of any meal.

Finally, they found themselves in a small chamber, seated in a close circle of couches and chairs. Tym centered himself on a stool in front of a deep fireplace. The castle seemed to have a chill these past couple nights, so Tym lit a Peckwood fire. The blue-green flames splashed light around the otherwise dark room.

Tym put a small lamp on a stand next to him. Olena guessed he needed the light to read from the ancient-looking, oversized book on his lap. This orange glow contrasted with the Peckwood flames and made her friends faces silhouettes against the shimmering walls draped with shadows.

Olena looked around the circle. To her right sat Ovara, then Dew sharing a couch with

Zandria and Adam. Eisenhahn occupied another couch with tiny Sylvan, who apparently gave up his Rockhorn body for the evening. Then came Tym and lastly Kez sat on the floor to her immediate left.

Everyone looked ready.

"Before I begin," started Tym, as he laid the book flat on his lap, "let me tell you that these accounts are documented from the First Queen herself, nearly one hundred years after the events actually happened."

"Does that mean they're not true?" asked Dew.

"It means what I read may not be exactly as it happened. However, I suspect much of it to be fairly accurate, as my mother told me her part when I was an elfling," said Tym.

"Are you gonna start the story now?" asked Adam.

Tym looked a little surprised by his directness. "Yes, of course."

He opened the thick cover and Olena thought she saw some gold dust wisp up into the air. That could have been a trick of the light though, she admitted.

"This is the story of the first four queens of Empyrean," Tym continued. "It is the story of the end of the Immortals and the beginning of Empyrean. It is the return of a long Forgotten Evil and the arrival of a stranger. True there are four queens, but first there was only one. No one knows exactly from where or when she came."

The room felt unnaturally quiet as Tym spoke. Each listener seemed so intent that Olena thought they stopped breathing. The only other sound came from the comforting crackle of the fire. Olena felt suspended in Tym's web of words and could almost picture the story in her mind.

Tym said, "It is believed the First Queen witnessed the last battle of the Immortals and the Fall of Gilgamesh. Some say she was there when the dark lieutenants freed their master, the Forgotten Evil, from his mystical prison. The enchanted black stone prison shattered and flew from the Central Plains to each of the four realms. One of these pieces landed at the eastern edge of Empyrean. There is where the First Queen of the Eastern Sky came into Empyrean. At that time, she was known only as Nyssa the Traveler."

Chapter 3

The First King

Nyssa felt like she had been asleep. *Good*, she thought, *only a dream. But what a strange dream?* She remembered the giants, all fighting. She remembered the black rock and something inside it. Something long forgotten.

She rolled over on her unusually hard bed and felt a gentle breeze on her face. She guessed she must have left the window open.

With that thought, Nyssa's mind honed in on several facts all at once. The sudden realizations forced her sleepy eyes open. In the instant that it took her eyelids to move up, Nyssa recounted everything that happened to her. She remembered her foster parents smoldering house, the odd shop keeper, the giant men fighting the giant monsters, the thing inside the black rock and the blast that sent her reeling backwards.

She associated that last thought with the sensation of flying. With her eyes open and focused, Nyssa discovered she was flying. Somehow, she got caught up with one of the quarters of the shattered rock. The force of the blast must have lifted her up and the shockwave knocked her unconscious. Now she found herself lying on the flat surface of the rock, soaring through the air. The wind in her hair reminded her of the bike she had when she was ten. She only had it for two months, but she could go fast. This seemed faster.

Nyssa could not see the ground when she looked over the edge. She had never been this high, not even on an airplane. For that matter, she had never been on any airplane. The height terrified her for an instant, but then it unexpectedly turned into fun. The rock did not teeter or roll. It simply zipped along. Never in her life had Nyssa felt such peaceful solitude. Only the whooshing sound of the rock cutting through the air reached her ears. She did not think birds could possibly fly this high.

Then something did come into view. Nyssa could see the purple and gray tips of what had to be mountains. Much like an airplane, Nyssa had never seen mountains in person. The jagged spires raced by and for a brief moment, she could see the ridges and passes stretch out below her. And as fast as they appeared, the peaks disappeared behind her.

Everything went back to that peaceful quiet.

Nyssa did not give any thought to where or when she might land. Instead, her thoughts went back to her arrival in this strange place. She knew it was not her home. She did not even think it was Earth. She ran through a door at the back of a curiosity shop and ended up here.

Karl Lumpkin.

That was the man's name. He said he opened a doorway home. *If not to her home*, Nyssa thought, *this must be his home*. Nyssa had a hard time trusting very many adults. However, in her few seconds with Mr. Lumpkin, he seemed completely trustworthy. She almost felt bad for running through his shop and messing with his door, but she had her own problems. She recalled him saying the door would only work for one person. After seeing the monsters that lived in this place, she sort of wished she could trade places with him.

Too late for that, she thought.

After going through the door, Nyssa almost got squished in the middle of a battle. Even in the confusion, she easily could tell the difference between what she called the good guys and the bad guys. She hoped she never had to see those slimy, three-eyed creeps again.

The others did not make her feel much better, though. At least the three that did not run away tried to protect her. The one called Para-whatever reminded her of a dinosaur. Nyssa felt like the one called Horus should have meant something more to her. Maybe she had heard his name before, like in a history book or something, she mused.

She liked the tallest one with the white beard best. He seemed very much like a father should be. He was strong and protected her with his own body. She knew he had to be wise, too. She based this conclusion on his looks and nothing else.

The one that looked like his younger brother made her angry though. She did not like that he ran away from the fight. She did not like fighting, but she thought running away from trouble was worse. That is when she realized she had a lot in common with this giant. She ran away from her own troubles, which landed her in this confusing world. This realization made her angry at herself.

Nyssa could feel the rock starting to descend, which brought her mind to her present situation. She had nothing to hold on to when she landed, but she did not have to worry about that yet. Below her, she could now see what looked like an endless expanse of lush, green forest.

Then something strange happened.

Nyssa felt literally and physically beside herself. She looked at her hand and saw, not one, but two sets of fingers. The ten fingers instantly became twenty, forty, more than she could count. Everything in sight blurred like a shuffling deck of cards. As her hand spread out and multiplied, she now watched it gradually fuse back into one hand. Nyssa did not feel any pain and knew her body did not really separate. The closest thing she could compare it to was spinning a coin on a table. For a moment, everything was a blur and heads was as good as tails. As the coin would slow, in the moments before it fell flat, she could see each side trading places. Nyssa felt like that coin now, as if she somehow traded places with herself.

With everything calm again, Nyssa looked back at the ground. The beautiful, thriving forest looked dead and rotted. She saw a massive creature perched on a dilapidated building.

A dragon, Nyssa screamed in her head.

Beneath the dragon, at the center intersection of the small town, she saw a man on the back of a black horse talking to what seemed to be a crowd of animals.

Then the blurring, shuddering vision returned. When it stopped, the forest was green again. No town, no animals, no dragon.

The rock continued its decline on a downward slant.

The forest hastily turned into a jungle. From the ground, Nyssa suspected the transition might seem more gradual. From her height and speed, however, one moment it was a broadleaf forest and the next, a palm tree jungle.

She could hear the underside of the rock shredding the wide palms leaves as she dipped lower. Wet flakes of green sprayed up on either side. She could hear the surprised cries of what had to be birds or other tree-dwelling jungle creatures.

Then she cleared the jungle and rapidly fell onto a reddish-brown beach. She skimmed the chunky surface, unable to tell if it was sand or rock. Nyssa's flight ended with a jolt that tossed her forward. She never took the time to look for handholds and paid the price for her lack of preparation. She flew off the shiny black rock, flipped in the air and landed on her back in the water.

The disorientation scared her into thinking she was drowning. Nyssa embarrassingly discovered the water was only waist deep. She stopped her flailing and planted her tennis shoes in the wet sand. Why do I keep getting wet, she wondered.

In front of her, an ocean seemed to stretch on forever. Behind her, the black rock embedded into the shore, its flat surface sticking out like a ledge over the water. Now she could see the beach to be covered by dull, jagged brown rocks, ripe with algae.

Something down the beach caught her eye. A man, a giant man, stood in the water staring out at the sea. It looked like the giant that ran away from the fight.

Before she could be sure, her vision shifted again in the same blurry way. This time, she lost her balance and plopped down in the water. She seemed to be in the same spot, but the man was gone and the air felt a little warmer. As a result of losing her balance, Nyssa fell below the edge of the rock and stayed put. She believed it to be safest because she thought she heard someone above her now. She did not want any of those smoky giants to find her if they were looking for the brown-bearded man.

Nyssa carefully peeked up from her hiding place. She saw a boy sitting with a powerful-looking black horse, similar to the one she saw in the village during her flight. She thought they were talking to each other. For the second time, she thought a human was talking to an animal. Of course, if she saw a real dragon, then would talking to animals be any more unusual, she asked herself. The boy threw a chunk of bread in her direction and Nyssa quickly ducked. A seagull swooped down and snagged the crumb, but did not seem to notice her.

Nyssa huddled under the lip of the black rock with water lapping at her soaked feet while the boy, horse and bird finished their picnic. They seemed to be talking about something important, but she could not hear them clearly. She did not dare peek again until she was sure they were a safe distance away. When she finally looked out, she saw the boy, with his back to her, riding the horse. The boy studied a map as he rode out of sight, the bird following behind them in the air.

The blurring vision started and Nyssa said, "Here we go again."

When it stopped, everything looked the same, except no boy, no horse, no bird.

"You came back," said a deep voice behind her.

Nyssa spun around to see the dark haired giant approaching. She had nowhere to go, so she decided to confront him.

"And?" said Nyssa defensively.

The giant looked down at her. He stroked his rough looking beard for a moment, then put his hands on his hips.

Finally, he said, "After our certain defeat, I did not expect you to return."

Nyssa let her anger get the better of her despite their incomprehensible size difference. She shouted, "They probably wouldn't have lost if you didn't run away."

She knew her behavior was not any better than his, but she doubted he knew that.

A massive hand snatched her by the front of her shirt and Nyssa hung in front of the man helplessly. She looked into his angered face, hoping he did not plan to eat her.

"How dare you accuse Gilgamesh, King of Kings, of cowardice. I ruled millions and defeated armies before coming to this hopeless place. I stood by Odin as he tore this world asunder to form a new land. I am no coward."

With her feet dangling in the air, Nyssa felt she had no choice but to figuratively stand her ground. She asked, "Why did you run after the rock broke open?"

Gilgamesh pulled her closer. His breath smelled stale, like an old museum. He said, "I did not run in fear. At least not fear of my enemy. The Forgotten Evil cast our weapon away. There is but one thing in all worlds that will defeat him and now it, the Atumval, has been lost beyond the sea."

He gently returned Nyssa to the ground before speaking again. She thought he looked more sad than angry now.

"I tried to recover the Atumval," he continued. "Unfortunately, *his* power pushed it beyond my reach. Even with the fastest ship, I might never find it beyond this vast sea. Worse still, what if it landed in the water and not on ground?"

"But you left your friends alone," said Nyssa. She chided herself for such big talk from someone that avoided making friends.

Gilgamesh stared at the ocean. He said, "I do not know from where you came, but I am certain you do not belong here."

At least he got that right, she thought to herself. Standing in soggy shoes did not help her mood and Nyssa felt like arguing.

"You don't know anything about me," she said.

He stepped past her to examine the shiny black rock with its metallic silver speckles. Nyssa wondered if he was going to ignore her comment.

Gilgamesh finally said, "True, as much as you know nothing about me."

But, thought Nyssa, she did. At least, she felt like she was supposed to. The giant attempted to move the stone, but nothing happened. The rock looked only to be about the length of his arm and should have been easy to lift by someone of his perceived strength. Still, he could not move it. It seemed to be permanently embedded on this shore.

"I was a king," he said again, mostly to himself.

Gilgamesh climbed on top of the stone and peered at the jungle. From her vantage, Nyssa guessed he could see over the tops of the swaying palms trees with no difficulty. He turned and looked up the shore, then down the shore. Eventually, he turned back to face the ocean.

"There looks to be a village not too far off to the south," he said, pointing down the shore. "Go there for food and shelter. The natives of this land are foolishly accepting. I do not expect you will see me again. I am going in search of the Atumval."

The talk of the Atumval intrigued Nyssa. She wanted to know more about it, but her vision blurred again and Gilgamesh was gone. Nyssa saw no other choice but to head toward the small village by the sea.

Chapter 4

The First Village

Having tennis shoes on this rocky beach made her thankful, even though they were soaked. Nyssa could not imagine walking across the sharp red-brown rocks barefoot. She carefully followed the direction Gilgamesh showed her, moving away from the unpleasant black rock.

Nyssa felt like she was heading down the shore. However, as she watched the sun begin to set out over the ocean, she figured that to be the west and her course to be north, up shore. She noticed Gilgamesh called it south though, which would mean the sun was setting in the east. That made no sense to her, but nothing in this place had so far.

She found a narrow path near the edge of the jungle which relieved her from the uneven, broken rocks. This made her walking seem to go much faster. She hoped she would be there before dark. To her disappointment, Nyssa saw absolutely no sign of it.

Along her walk, Nyssa's vision blurred three more times. She started calling this "the switch" because everything switched around her each time she refocused. Sometimes, the changes were minor, like a tree growing from small to big. Other times, major things happened, like Gilgamesh disappearing.

These three switches qualified as incredible by Nyssa's standards. First, she stood in front of a magnificent sand castle. It looked brand new and big enough for a hundred people to live in it. A worker balanced at the top of a bamboo ladder, scraping and shaping the upper curve of the wide entrance. He worked the sand with a tool that looked like a seashell until the surface was extremely smooth. The amazing look of the castle could easily have been created by the wind as by any worker. Nyssa thought the wavy walls and swirly pillars could not possibly be all made by hand.

"Do you like it?" a voice asked next to her.

Nyssa thought she was alone and she thought she was hidden by the edge of the jungle. The surprising voice came from her right as if the person walked out of the jungle.

She turned to face a pretty young woman. Nyssa guessed she could not be much older than herself. The woman stood bare foot, wearing a short, simple white dress that looked perfect for a day at the beach.

"What?" said Nyssa.

"My name is Remina and that is my palace. Do you like it?" repeated the woman.

Before Nyssa could tell her yes, that she did love the beautiful palace by the sea, the switch came again. Remina disappeared right in front of her.

When Nyssa turned around, she saw ruins where the brand new castle was a moment ago. She had a hard enough time trying to make sense of people appearing and disappearing. This did not make sense. How could the castle go from being new to being instantly destroyed? She thought about the trees changing size too. She thought it would take years for a tree to grow and even longer for a castle to fall apart. Even if someone purposely destroyed the castle, it could not happen instantly.

Then Nyssa considered the ocean. Although things changed on the land, the ocean did not seem to change with each switch. It seemed constant, continuous. She had only ever seen the ocean in movies or text books, but she wondered if the sea could ever change.

This made Nyssa think that maybe things around her were not changing, maybe she was? Could it be that she disappeared in front of the woman and not the other way around, she hypothesized. Nyssa remembered Gilgamesh remarking that she *came back*.

An approaching noise interrupted her from pondering it any longer. Nyssa looked down a long road she had not noticed before. It led directly to the once inspiring castle gate. In the distance, a carriage pulled by two powerful black horses came toward her at a casual pace. Two more horses with riders followed behind the carriage.

Nyssa ducked into the undergrowth before she was spotted. She watched through the broad green leaves. As the carriage passed, she could see inside. The passengers were three old women and some kids, the youngest had countless, amusing curls.

She thought the curly-haired girl looked directly at her, but then the third switch happened. Alone, Nyssa crouched at the edge of the jungle. No carriage, no road, no palace. The sun dipped closer to the line of the sea on the horizon. In the dimming light, it looked as if the giant sand castle had never existed.

Without the castle blocking her view, Nyssa could make out a slope where the ugly rocks ended. She deliberately crossed the wide open space. The sound of her footsteps startled something that looked like a crab and it scuttled back into the water. From the top of the slope, which turned out to be more like a wall separating the shale from the sand, Nyssa could see a small village. So small, she only counted six huts. At the far end, a group of people huddled near a dwindling fire.

The sight of the warm flames made Nyssa aware of how cold she had become after being soaked. Her soggy clothes and the salty ocean breeze made her want to be down with the strangers. In her present condition, she did not care what kind of people they were, as long as they were warm. Once she got close, she almost changed her mind. They looked like cavemen, or maybe Australian aborigines, like she learned about in World History. Either way, they looked a little frightening to her by the fading flicker of the fire.

Luckily, their unsettling appearance did not match their welcoming behavior. They graciously widened their close circle and made a space for Nyssa to get warm.

"Thanks," she said, fairly certain they could not understand her. She assumed they did not speak her language.

One of the older men responded to her thanks, though, with a guttural sound. To Nyssa, it almost sounded like he was clearing his throat. He pointed at her, then at the fire. After that, he slowly waved his hand over their village like he was presenting it to her.

Nyssa managed to warm up before the shivers started. After a few minutes, she felt comfortable enough to try and communicate with them. This was the first time she was around people that were not trying to hurt each other or disappear. Maybe, she hoped, she could get something from them about this strange place into which she stumbled.

She asked, "Where am I?"

No response.

She figured they could not understand her. Then the elder gave her an answer in his native tongue that sounded like clicks and grunts. Nyssa wondered if he understood her. She tried to repeat his sounds, but it came out like, "Ba-nook-a-nook?"

"Ba-nook-nook," responded the elder with a grin.

"That's it. Banookanook," Nyssa said again. Nyssa liked the sound of her new word. It seemed like a good name for this village.

Apparently the natives liked it too. They repeated the word as best they could while laughing and eating. The elder offered Nyssa some of their meal.

She suddenly realized how hungry she was and began eating without looking at the food. She soon discovered it to be some kind of raw fish. Nyssa shrugged away the surprise of it and kept eating. Her hunger outweighed her gag reflex at the moment. She did wonder why they would eat raw food if they knew how to make a fire, though. Maybe they have not learned to cook yet, she guessed.

While she finished her meal, the seventeen villagers began singing. One of the women started to chant and several children joined her. By the time Nyssa chewed her last bite, everyone joined in on the song.

Nyssa loved music and this unusual sound was no exception. She had no idea what the words meant. She did not even try to guess. She almost could not hear the low chanting over the lapping of the nearby waves. Still, this strange, beautiful sound seemed to work in harmony with the ocean. The rhythm of the waves rolled with their voices, like part of the song. Nyssa guessed the simple villagers must have learned to sing by listening to the water.

She wanted to join them, to sing like she did when she was alone, doing dishes or walking home after school. Something in her heart, anger or frustration, kept her from finding the melody. Somehow that thing inside the black rock seemed to steal the music from her. She wanted it back, but did not know what to do about it. Nyssa sat in silence, listening to a song she hoped would not end. She wished she could stay here forever.

Of course, *the switch* changed that.

Chapter 5

The First Immortal

When Nyssa regained her focus, she saw no sign of the villagers or their fire in front of her. She stood up to look at the small village behind her. Something new replaced it. Instead of six simple huts made from giant seashells, she saw three rows of huts, twenty in all. They still had some walls made from the strange spiky shells, but also wood frames and cloth curtains hanging in the windows. Behind that, up above the rock slope, the sand castle returned and it looked amazing.

Thousands of candles decorated the palace with multi-colored flames. They lined the tops of the walls, windows and surrounded the main gate. Even the full moon over the ocean paled in comparison to this magnificent display.

From the light of the moon, Nyssa could see similar decorations in Banookanook as well. Most of the candles had burned down, but she also saw painted shells hung on strings between the huts. She guessed this had to represent some kind of holiday.

Then Nyssa saw something else. A black shape darted between two of the huts. She immediately thought of the horrible monsters fighting over the black rock, but she reassured herself this one was much smaller. Another black shape bounced from roof to roof. It stopped on the hut closest to her. Although these were not the three eyed giants, her reassurance faded as they came closer.

This black figure looked like a skinny boy, except not quite a boy. It stared at her with an eyeless face. The creature not only did not have eyes, but no nose, mouth or hair. Under the moonlight and shimmer from the palace, Nyssa could see the creature's smooth black head adorned with two pointy ears. It turned its head to put one of those ears in her direction.

Nyssa did not make a sound.

Whatever these things were, she knew there were more than two. She caught glimpses of the mysterious boy-like creatures dodging between and dashing over the huts. They seemed to be looking for something.

She watched the one in front of her. It leapt to the ground and headed down the row of huts, partly crawling, partly running. It went directly to a giant figure that Nyssa had not noticed until this moment.

Nyssa knew this giant man with his long white beard. She thought Gilgamesh called him Odin. He looked mostly the same as when she first saw him on the plains. He still had long white hair and intricate braids in his full white beard. He stood tall, looked muscular and maybe a little tired, but not any older. Nyssa thought he somehow seemed ancient and yet childish at the same time. He had a gleam in his eye as if his heart was filled with joy and it shone out of him. Maybe, Nyssa thought, that could be the reflection from the candles too. The man no longer looked ready for battle. He wore clean, deep green robes, stretching to the ground, trimmed with red silk. He also carried a thick walking stick almost as tall as he was.

One of the black creatures next to him carried a large sack that looked stuffed full. Nyssa guessed the little black creatures to be unnaturally strong if one of them could carry something so big with apparent ease. The old giant reached into the sack and took out a single decorated object. A present, thought Nyssa. She watched him reach as far as he could inside the nearest hut and leave the present without disturbing anybody sleeping inside.

The boyish thing that spotted Nyssa now caught the giant's attention. The giant knelt like a teacher next to a student's desk. They looked to be communicating, but Nyssa could not imagine how the small one could do that without a mouth. She did not hear a sound from either of them until the giant stood.

He patted the little one on the head and said to him, "Thank you. I know, but it is not quite her time yet."

Both of them turned in her direction and Nyssa ducked behind a hut, almost cutting herself on the intriguing spiked shell that made up the wall of this hut. Then she heard the big man speaking to someone else.

Nyssa peeked out to see a tiny girl talking rather boldly to the enormous man. She looked close to four years old and more than a little upset.

"I don't want it, I don't want the baby," she said.

The giant scooped up the little girl with one huge hand. He said, "Let me tell you a secret, you are going to have a baby sister soon. Your parents have more than enough love in their hearts for both you and your new sister. This is the time when we are supposed to be thankful for all of our gifts. Things will change for you soon and then you will have the most important job and your friendship with your sister will be greater than any gift I could ever give you."

Nyssa moved back into hiding. She pressed her back against the hut and closed her eyes to keep from crying. She would do anything for a real family and this selfish little girl was complaining about getting a new sister. Nyssa fought back tears of loneliness. She hoped that the little girl would come to love her sister, but from the sound of it, that would take a miracle.

After another minute, Nyssa opened her eyes only to have a huge face fill her vision. The giant somehow traveled the length of the village in the few seconds that she closed her eyes. He bent low to make eye contact with her.

He said, "Now it is your time."

He rose up and Nyssa saw herself surrounded by the black creatures. Nyssa's heart caught in her throat.

The giant must have understood the look of concern on her face. He said, "Don't worry, child. The Pitirs will not harm you as long as there is some goodness in your heart."

"The Pitirs?" asked Nyssa. "Who are you?"

"The Pitirs are my helpers. You may call me Father Odin," he said.

She knew Gilgamesh called him Odin. Maybe, she wondered, Odin did not recognize her. Then she became aware that he did remember her with his next words.

Odin said, "I feared we lost you when the stone split all those years ago."

Years ago? Nyssa did not believe it. "What do you mean?"

"It may seem a little complicated, Nyssa," he said.

"How do you know my name?" she demanded.

"You told it to me the first time we met," Odin explained.

Confusion tried to take over Nyssa's mind.

"When did we meet? Please start making sense." Nyssa did not want him to know she was getting scared.

"Why, almost two thousand years ago," said Odin. "Don't you remember coming to Empyrean?"

Empyrean? Is that what they called this place, she wondered. She knew it was not her own world, so it had to have some name. In her world, the sun did not set backwards and animals did not talk. Thus far, Nyssa did not much like this place called Empyrean. She felt something bad was happening here.

Father Odin sat on the ground next to her. The ground seemed to shudder under his weight and then settled. He patted his knee and said, "Please, sit and I will explain."

Nyssa reluctantly climbed up on his lap. It oddly reminded her of going to the shopping mall at Christmas. She got to sit on Santa's lap once. The black Pitirs slinked off into the shadows, leaving her alone with Odin.

He continued, "I found a barren place that needed life. So, I tore open the ground, leaving cliffs and canyons in the west and high mountains in the east. The land unrolled out to the sea. This beach here is the very spot I held onto as I pulled and stretched Empyrean into existence. In the middle of this beautiful place, I found a black rock. I believe you know of which I speak."

Nyssa nodded. She had no words for this fanciful story. She did dare to think his magical touch caused this beach to be different than the rest of the rocky coastline.

"This Forgotten Evil created itself in perfect balance with the Atumval. Do you know of the Atumval?" asked Odin. He waited only long enough for Nyssa to give a brief sign of recognition. "They existed together before time and creation. At some point before I walked in this world, the darkness gained self-awareness and tried to defeat the light. This struggle caused all worlds to explode into existence. Neither one of these forces is supposed to exist within reality and it is here that one can destroy the other."

The talk of creating worlds and a balance of good and evil made Nyssa's head spin. She knew of the Atumval only because Gilgamesh called it by the same name. Too much of this story sounded familiar, but all called by different names where she came from. Odin did not give her a chance to ask any questions.

"Some time before you arrived, the Atumval must have sealed away the long Forgotten Evil in that rock. For an immeasurable time, we Immortals fought against the Forgotten Evil's lieutenants to keep him trapped. Your arrival, your energy, gave the darkness the advantage it needed to break free."

"I'm sorry. I didn't know," said Nyssa. She always seemed to be getting blamed for something.

Odin said, "It is not your fault. Everything happens as it should. Besides, I'm sure Karl knew."

Karl? Nyssa thought of the man that opened the door which led her to Empyrean. She asked, "You mean the shopkeeper?"

"He is that and more," said Odin. "Don't worry, you will see him again. He has a knack for coming and going. Now about your problem..."

"What problem?" Nyssa interrupted.

Odin looked at her sternly. Nyssa instantly felt bad for talking to him like that.

"You have a problem of stability," said Odin. "You were much to close to the Forgotten Evil and absorbed back more energy than he took from you. This surplus has caused you to lose your anchor in time. Maybe you have noticed this already, but you will bounce back and forth through time until the energy is spent."

She had noticed it. Traveling through time completely explained the changing trees, castles and people. "I call it *the switch*," she said.

"Ha, the switch," laughed Odin. "I forgot. How clever! While you are not from this world, you will have to start obeying its rules. As such, we will have to get you back to your starting point. You are needed there. I can show you an easy way to do that."

Before Odin could finish, Nyssa's vision blurred and she switched to a new time.

Chapter 6

The First Interruption

"You made that up," said Adam.

"I was going to say that," added Dew.

Everyone started talking at once about Tym's remarkable tale.

Olena thought it sounded amazing. She could not believe the First Queen came from another world. She barely knew anything about her own world. The idea of whole other worlds excited her. Tym did not say much about the other place, but the little he did say sounded kind of scary. Maybe when Queen Nyssa finally wrote of her adventures, she might have forgotten all but the worst things about her original home.

Adam stood up and said, "I'm supposed to believe she was hiding under the same rock where I found Crumb?"

"I can only tell you what is on the page," said Tym. He looked offended, thought Olena. "I most certainly did not make up this story. Please understand that the Deep Magic affected the First Queen greatly. When she first arrived in Empyrean, she travelled forward and backward through time. It is certainly possible that she was there."

Adam appeared satisfied with the answer. However, Olena had another question. She clicked her tongue against her teeth in a way that had become quite well known.

She said, "I know Father Odin is supposed to deliver presents every Queen's Day. But I never knew he was real. Is Father Odin one of the Immortals?"

Zandria answered before Tym could, "I think it is him. I remember meeting him that night. I always believed it was a dream."

Olena thought her sister looked on the verge of tears.

Dew still did not look convinced.

"Now hold on," said the younger elf. "You're telling us that these two sisters have met three of the four Immortals? Next you'll be telling us that my grandmother was there."

"And my mother," said Tym. "Remember, they are twin sisters and they fought in the First War for Empyrean. But don't get ahead of the story."

"Yes, but the Immortals are only legends, like the Atumval," said Dew.

"I believe in them," offered Olena.

Kez climbed up on her lap. He said, "According to the legend, the Immortals left Empyrean when the first queens came into power. They never found the Atumval, that I know of. I do have some difficulty believing both Horus and the Parasauratitan are Immortals."

"But Karl said they were," Olena added defensively.

The mention of her missing friend stung her heart. She mostly tried to avoid thinking about Karl, because she always feared what happened to him. She tried to change the subject, "Kez, you never told me about this Atumval thing."

"I always thought it was make believe," said Kez. "Now, I'm not so sure. The Nookans have a few stories of their own about the sea and other ancient things."

Another round of everyone talking at the same time pushed these thoughts from Olena's head.

Kez spoke the loudest, "Alright. If Tym purports this story to be true, then I believe him. With the possibility of *time travel*, we should prepare ourselves for more interesting meetings and coincidences. It seems that great people and events have a way of drawing magic to them. I shall not be surprised to find this Nyssa drawn to Olena at some point. But please don't tell me she is going to appear in front of us."

Tym shifted on his seat. He looked ready to continue reading. Finally, he said, "I will not tell you that, but, of course, I've read this story before and know how it ends."

Chapter 7

The First Mother

Nyssa felt like she would never get used to the switch. Every time, it blurred her vision and upset her stomach. Mostly, she thought it felt like motion sickness, although she did not move at all.

Or did she?

Her feet did not move, but according to Odin, she moved through time. Nyssa had seen that new movie about a time traveling car and read a few time travel books, but she knew it could not be possible.

Then she corrected herself. It could not be possible in the world she knew. She traveled into a fantastic new world. She left her home and came to Empyrean. So far, she met two giants and was fairly certain she saw a dragon. *Why, anything could be possible in this crazy place,* she imagined.

When Nyssa regained her vision, she looked around the beach. The sun slowly rose over the jungle, reflecting brilliantly off the churning waves. She thought a moment about Gilgamesh's directions. He had sent her south, which to her, meant the sun had to be coming up in the west. First it sets in the wrong direction and now it rises in the wrong direction.

"What a mixed up world," Nyssa said to herself.

As she surveyed the rest of Banookanook, she thought about Odin's last words.

He said she had to get back to her starting point. She guessed that meant where she first came to Empyrean. She recalled the river and the wide plains and the black rock.

The thought of the rock made her shudder.

She only vaguely felt it at first, but now definitely knew something evil had been inside that rock.

A Forgotten Evil.

Then, of course, it exploded and sent her flying. Nyssa had no idea how far she went. She had no idea how long it would take to get back there. She really had no guess where *there* was, except that it had to be west of where she now stood. From the beach, she realized, she could only go in one possible direction. It had to be west.

Lost in her thoughts, Nyssa did not pay attention to her wandering. She walked into the center of the huts that made up this version of Banookanook. If any of the villagers came along, they would spot her instantly. She lost the safety of her hiding place.

A quick look at the melted down candles and slightly faded decorations told her another Queen's Day had passed. Could it be the same one as before her switch, Nyssa wondered. The trees did not look much different, neither did the huts nor the amazing sand palace in the distance.

To confirm her suspicion, the same little girl that talked with Odin about the new baby ran out of the hut right in front of Nyssa. She still looked about four years old.

As the sheet covering the doorway fell closed, Nyssa could hear a crying baby inside the hut. Now, Nyssa knew she had only traveled a few days into the future. The new baby from the late night encounter had been born.

Suddenly, the parents came out of the hut. Nyssa rapidly dashed for cover behind the next closest hut. From here, she could see the big sister playing down by the water and hear the parents talking. No one seemed to notice her though.

In the glimpse she caught of the father, he looked almost identical to the natives she met last night. At least it was last night for her. For all she knew, thousands of years could have passed for the village. The father had the same dark skin as the ancient villagers and the same thick curly hair. His face looked heartbroken and defeated. Nyssa wondered why a new father would look that way. His words told her why.

He said, "Kisa, you can't leave now. I need you. The girls need you."

The woman called Kisa looked nothing like the man. She stood tall and elegant with long, wavy brown hair. She carried her slender frame with grace and never let the hem of her simple white dress brush the sand.

Kisa said, "My darling Apari, it is time for me to go. Queen Remina has read the signs and feels that I may one day be her replacement."

Apari interrupted, "We've gone over this. I know it is only supposed to be for a short time, but we haven't even named the baby yet."

Nyssa had heard plenty of arguing parents. She tuned out the sound and stared at the little girl splashing in the waves. Nyssa wished she could be that carefree and happy some day.

Then Kisa said something that snapped Nyssa back to attention.

"I am going west and will be back before you know it."

The West.

Nyssa needed to go west. A hundred thoughts dashed through her mind. Maybe she could follow this woman or maybe she could make friends with her and they could travel together?

"Tell Zandria goodbye for me," said Kisa. "If I tell her myself, she will never let me go. Also, kiss Olena."

Apari said, "Olena?"

"Yes. I think we should call her Olena. It means *shining light*. I have a feeling that someday she will be a light for all of Empyrean," said Kisa.

Then the tall woman walked away without another word.

Nyssa did not want the father to see her. She ducked low behind the hut and headed for the jungle. She made it to the tree line as the mother, Kisa, climbed the rock wall at the north end of the beach. Nyssa followed quietly, not sure whether she should make herself known to the woman.

She focused ahead of herself as she walked. Nyssa did not see the furry tail sticking out of the bushes until she stepped on it. The wild looking creature squealed and vanished into the jungle. What little she saw of it, Nyssa thought it looked like a monkey, except it had the face of an old man with a puff of unkempt white hair on top.

The sound of the jungle animal caused Kisa to look directly at her. Nyssa had nowhere to go.

"Hello, child," said the woman.

"Um, hi," answered Nyssa, slightly embarrassed.

"Well don't stand there. Come to me," ordered Kisa.

The tone of her voice sounded friendly and irresistible. Nyssa felt like she had no other choice. For a brief moment, she thought she might follow the monkey-like thing into the jungle to hide. However, Kisa had such a presence that Nyssa instinctively obeyed. Kisa did not seem mean or angry. Nyssa recognized some quality in this mother that made it natural for others to respond positively to her.

Nyssa slowly made her way to the woman, who now stood at the edge of a small market.

Nyssa did not remember seeing this the last time she had been in front of the palace.

"It seems you frightened a quzzak," said Kisa.

"I stepped on his tail," admitted Nyssa.

Kisa looked toward the jungle. Compassion filled her face. She put a hand on Nyssa's shoulder.

Kisa said, "That sounded like Kez. He's had his tail pulled more than once by my Zandria. You didn't hurt him. Now, tell me what you are doing sneaking around Banookanook? You look a long way from home."

With Kisa's hand still on her shoulder, they walked into the market. Nyssa realized that the woman knew she had been outside their hut. She knew she had to tell the truth. Before Nyssa could speak, a few merchants greeted Kisa with great respect. The woman kindly waved back to them. Nyssa began to feel a trust with this woman. She also felt something that she had yet to experience in this land of Empyrean.

Peace.

Nyssa felt peace coming from Kisa. It made her momentarily forget all of the outrageous things that had happened to her in the past twenty four hours. Somehow, it seemed that she was right where she was supposed to be.

Then Kisa took her hand from Nyssa's shoulder. Immediately, Nyssa's vision blurred. She could feel the switch coming.

Kisa grabbed her hand and said, "You're not going anywhere."

The switch stopped as quickly as it started. Everything remained exactly the same. Nyssa did not travel anywhere this time. Apparently, Kisa did not want her to go yet.

They held hands as they walked out of the market along the wide road that cut a path into the jungle. Nyssa did not want to let go of Kisa for fear of switching again. The warm, soft hand with the slender fingers easily wrapped around her own hand. Love came through that gentle grip, up Nyssa's arm and into her heart. She had not known this kind of love since the last time her birth mother held her too many years ago.

Although they had been walking long enough to be out of sight of the palace and the market, Kisa said, "You should walk with me."

"I am," answered Nyssa.

"And I am glad. I have a long journey ahead of me and I want you to stay with me," said Kisa.

"Where are we going?" asked Nyssa.

"I am going to Castle Empyrean beyond the Euphoric Mountains. I am not sure where you are going," said Kisa.

Nyssa wanted to tell this woman everything. Instead, she said, "I have to get back to the start. Father Odin said there was an easy way, but I don't know which way that is."

"Oh," said Kisa. "You spoke with Odin?"

"You don't believe me?" said Nyssa. She usually had to defend herself to adults. She wondered if it would be any different with Kisa.

And thankfully, it was different.

Kisa said, "I do believe you. Only, it's been quite a long time since he's spoken to anyone. When did you see him?"

"First at the black rock, fighting. Then in your village. A few days ago, I think," said Nyssa.

"You witnessed the Battle of the Black Stone?" asked Kisa. She looked shocked and for the first time, not at peace.

Nyssa thought she said something wrong. She did not want Kisa to be upset with her. She said, "Yes, but only for a moment. I don't stay in the same time for very long. Did I do something wrong?"

Kisa regained her composure. The sense of peace and tranquility returned. She said, "No dear, you did nothing wrong. I will venture to say I know where you are going now."

This excited Nyssa. "Where?"

"With me," said Kisa. "To the crystal castle."

As they walked, their surroundings changed from jungle to forest. Kisa had so many questions for Nyssa that the younger girl could not ask any of her own. Kisa started by asking about Nyssa's peculiar footwear.

"They're called tennis shoes," explained Nyssa. "But I don't play tennis."

Then Nyssa had to explain the game of tennis. Kisa said they played a similar game at the Palace by the Sea sometimes. The conversation eventually turned to how Nyssa came to be in Empyrean.

Kisa said, "I've never met this Karl Lumpkin, but it doesn't sound like he makes mistakes. He must have had a reason for sending you here."

After that, Kisa wanted to know more about Nyssa's world. Nyssa told her about movies and fast food. Kisa looked sad when Nyssa told her that animals did not talk in her world.

Kisa explained, "Not all animals talk in Empyrean either. You can count on horses and birds. Many small animals can talk and a few types of the biggest ones. Fish and other water creatures almost never talk."

As quickly as the last traces of jungle gave way to the lonely forest, Nyssa heard a sound that did not belong to either the jungle or the forest. It sounded like a faint jingling. Kisa hushed Nyssa and they moved off to the side of the road.

The jingling gradually grew to a clanking sound. This sound made Nyssa hungry. It reminded her of banging pots and pans together when she was forced to do the dishes. Then a completely unpleasant sound snapped in between the rhythmic clinking. Nyssa recognized this sound from watching Civil War videos in history class.

The whip cracked again.

Eventually, something absurd rolled into sight. A small, miserable donkey pulled a wagon that seemed impossible because of its size. Nyssa thought the wagon looked more like a tall, skinny house rolling on tall, skinny wheels that should have broken under the weight. Pots and pans dangled from the side, chiming in unison with the donkey's chains as a far off warning of this wagon's approach.

The whip snapped again and Nyssa looked up at the apparently impatient driver.

Almost at the highest point of the tall, skinny wagon sat a tall, skinny man. He wore a tall, skinny hat that made him seem even taller. Nyssa could not believe the outrageous white suit that he wore, with a ruffled collar and cuffs to match his tall, skinny white hat.

The man pulled the long wooden brake lever. This caught the donkey by surprise. The poor creature gagged as the sudden stop pulled him backward.

"Ladies," said the man from atop his wagon. "Allow me to introduce myself. I am known across the north. I stupefy them in the south. I wonderfy them in the west." He winked at this. "Currently on an extended engagement in the enchanting east, I am master and host of the Carnivale Chaotica. I am Raymond Shaydaway."

All of the fancy talk did not impress Nyssa. The way his beard curled back toward his mouth made him look a little silly to her, especially with no moustache. Still, something about him made her uncomfortable. She looked to Kisa for a response.

Kisa did not say anything, but when they turned back to the wagon, Raymond Shaydaway stood on the ground. Nyssa knew there was no way he could have gotten down so fast. The small hairs on her arms stood up as he came closer.

"Would you care to see my carnival?" he asked.

"We would not," said Kisa with authority.

"That is too bad. I do have such delightfully terrible sights to show you," said Shaydaway.

"We should go," said Kisa. She urged Nyssa to move with a gentle shove.

Shaydaway stepped in front of them. He looked momentarily desperate, but then his showman's grin returned.

He said, "Please. Wait. For two lonely ladies on a lengthy stroll, one more moment of your time. I should like to show you a small piece of entertainment. If you will, a magic trick."

Nyssa heard a sharp click in the unsettling man's voice at the end of both magic and trick. He started to seem menacing and his professional tone wavered into something more sinister. Before she or Kisa could respond, Shaydaway displayed a slender crystal in his right hand. Nyssa did not see where it came from, but she guessed he must have had it up his sleeve.

Raymond Shaydaway danced the crystal through and around his fingers like a short wand. It spun and twinkled almost hypnotically. As Nyssa watched, she suddenly realized he had not one but two crystals. He somehow balanced and twirled both of them on one hand. They did not make a sound as they flipped sideways and spun around. No matter how fast he went, Shaydaway did not allow the crystals to touch.

Then he slowly raised his left hand. He held two more identical crystals, spinning them the same way as those in his right hand. When both hands looked level, he flipped his wrist. Instantly, the four crystals balanced on the tip of his right index finger, each one forming the side of a diamond shape. Nyssa guessed he was using magnets to make the shape, but she started to find herself enthralled regardless.

Shaydaway flicked his wrist again. One crystal flew up high in the air. Nyssa watched it and did not see the other three crystals in the palm of his hand as they tipped toward each other to form a miniature pyramid.

Nyssa watched the fourth crystal glide back down so that its pointed end could land on the top of the pyramid.

"Run," yelled Kisa as she forcefully pushed Nyssa out of the way.

A bright flash of blue light momentarily blinded Nyssa. As soon as she could see, she looked for Kisa. She could not see the woman anywhere, at first. She turned to Raymond Shaydaway and he looked hysterical, like a mad man.

"It worked! The Trammeler worked!" he cheered, staring at the four crystals clenched in his skinny fingers. He wrapped both fists tightly around them.

Inside each of the smoky crystals, Nyssa thought she could see Kisa staring out at her. She could see the woman's mouth move and a moment later heard her shouting to run. Nyssa knew she needed to get away, but she had one other thing to do first.

Nyssa charged at Shaydaway. At the same time, her vision started to blur. She could feel a switch coming and Kisa was not there to stop it.

"Not yet," Nyssa pleaded in her head.

She must have caught Shaydaway by surprise because she easily snatched the four crystals away from him. He started screaming at her.

A second later, Nyssa switched.

Shaydaway disappeared. His wagon and donkey vanished too. Nyssa looked at the crystals in her hands. She no longer saw an image of Kisa, only gray smoke swirled inside them now.

In the distance, Nyssa noticed a dirty bunch of little men coming her way.

"Dwarves?" she asked herself.

They carried a few bundles of cloth. Nyssa thought for a moment that the bundles might be babies. She could not imagine anyone treating babies so roughly. They even dropped one of the bundles and stepped on it, before picking it up again.

As the next switch came over her, Nyssa did not realize that she too dropped something.

After she vanished, she did not see one of the crystals lying in the road. She did not see one of the wicked, baby-napping dwarves pick it up to carry it on to their mines far below ground.

Chapter 8

The First Tear

Kez stroked his tail. He said, "I don't remember that."

Zandria stared at Olena.

She honestly had no memory of her younger sister's birth or their mother leaving. She always thought that they lost their mother when Olena was born because that was what their father told them. They did not learn the truth, at least in part, until the day they lost their father too.

Olena looked like she was going to cry. Zandria held out her arms. Olena rushed over to the couch and hugged her sister.

Both girls began crying.

Tym sat silently. Zandria thought he looked on the verge of tears as well.

Adam moved from the couch and took Olena's seat without a word. Zandria appreciated that he always seemed to know what she needed without her having to ask.

Olena sat in Adam's vacant seat next to her sister.

"That carnival guy was not very nice," said Eisenhahn.

Zandria remembered him and she remembered those crystals.

The Trammeler.

Zandria did not know what Olena and the other queens did with the Trammeler. She did not know they dropped it into the mists beneath Empyrean's Bell Chamber. She only hoped it was gone forever.

Zandria put her arm around Olena's shoulders. She said, "He's gone now and our mother is safe."

She did not know if she was trying to reassure Olena or herself with that statement. Then she fell quiet, waiting for Tym to continue the story.

Chapter 9

The First Fairies

Once her vision refocused, Nyssa still found herself on the forest path. She did not like being so exposed, but the only cover was the unexplored woods behind her.

She looked at the four smoky crystals in her hands, except that there were only three.

Three!

She obviously dropped one, but did not see it on the ground. Her feet had not moved. It had to be close to her. She realized if she dropped it before she switched, then she had no chance of finding it. Without the fourth crystal, she knew in her heart that she had no way of saving Kisa.

Nyssa tucked the three remaining crystals safely in her pockets, two on the left and one on the right. She decided to duck into the relative cover of the forest. She knew this would take her in the wrong direction from her goal, but she did not want to travel the road alone.

Inside, the mixed jungle and forest did not make her feel any safer. Nyssa felt like she was being constantly watched from the moment she left the road. She tried to concentrate on her direction. She did not want to lose which way was west.

She honestly did not think anyone could follow her through the tangled undergrowth, if someone was following her. She could not justify the feeling of mysterious eyes peering at her. She saw no proof, but after her experience with Shaydaway, Nyssa did not want to take any chances.

She walked away from the road, deeper into the jungle woods.

After walking for a while, it occurred to her that she should take the crystals back to Banookanook. She thought she should tell Apari what happened to his wife. Maybe he could take the crystals to that queen. She tried to remember what Kisa said her name was.

Queen Remina?

That was it. Remina. Nyssa remembered her now. She met Remina in front of the newly built palace during one of her first switches. Nyssa wondered for a moment how long ago that might have been.

Queen Remina struck Nyssa as intelligent and trustworthy, although she only stood with her for a moment. She hoped that the beautiful, young queen could save Kisa.

Nyssa looked at her surroundings. She had no clue which way it was to Banookanook. She did not pay enough attention and now did not know for sure which way led back to the road. She had to turn and duck to clear so many vines and branches that she could not say for certain she was even heading south.

She pushed through the next thick row of bushes and found herself in a wide clearing. The ring of trees only stood back far enough to give a narrow shore line to a beautiful, still lagoon. Nyssa could not believe the incredible waterfall that plummeted silently into the lagoon without making a single ripple.

"What is this place?" Nyssa asked aloud.

She stared up at the waterfall that came rapidly down from high atop a massive, jagged cliff wall.

"This is one of the sacred places of the east," answered a gentle voice.

Nyssa looked around, startled. She could not see anyone.

The voice continued, "Join us for a while. You need rest and some guidance."

Nyssa could not tell from where the voice came. Without a roar crashing down from the waterfall, the mysterious voice echoed across the entire lagoon.

From her encounter with Shaydaway, Nyssa now found it difficult to trust someone in hiding.

"Who are you?" demanded Nyssa.

The peaceful voice replied, "Come here and we will show you."

Then, a series of stones rose up from the bottom of the lagoon. Each looked perfectly circular and large enough for Nyssa to stand on its flat top. The stones broke the surface of the water, each about a wide step apart and they led in a straight line toward the continuous waterfall.

Nyssa felt compelled by the voice. She could not guess to whom, or what, it belonged. Her curiosity led her to find out the answer. Only a small part of her mind warned her it could be another trap. She felt mostly confident that the voice was friendly, but allowed a small possibility that it was not.

We? Nyssa realized the strange voice said *we will show you*. Before she stepped onto the first stone, Nyssa knew there was more than one person, or thing, waiting for her on the other side, although she could not see anything.

When her foot rested on the first stone, Nyssa felt it wobble. As soon as she planted her second foot, she looked into the clear water. The stone somehow floated on the surface of the water. Nyssa looked ahead and saw the others were the same. She thought they were tall rocks reaching up from the bottom, but the truth made no sense. Nyssa understood who, or whatever, she was about to meet had strong magic.

Nyssa took each step carefully. She did not want to get her shoes wet again so soon. They still felt squishy from the day before. Close to halfway across, Nyssa stopped to catch her balance. She looked into the deepest part of the lagoon and saw the muddy bottom strewn with gems of every color. They sparkled back at her, reassuring her that someone kind had to be waiting for her behind the waterfall.

Then the rushing torrent parted like a curtain. Nyssa could see a dark cave in the cliff face behind it. With each step closer, Nyssa could see flashes of color coming from deep within the darkness. When she leapt from the last floating stone to the mouth of the cave, the lights faded and the waterfall curtain closed behind her.

"Hello?" called Nyssa.

"Quietly, please," responded the constantly pleasant voice. "Come inside, but do it quietly."

The pitch black cave did not frighten Nyssa for a reason she could not quite identify. She walked into the darkness. After a moment, either her eyes adjusted to the dark or someone lit a very dim light. Nyssa could see a comfortable looking pile of pillows and cushions. A girl, younger than herself, lay sleeping in the middle.

A miniature woman in a red dress stepped up next to Nyssa. She must have been hiding, guessed Nyssa, because she did not see her a moment ago.

This woman said, "Please be quiet. Zandria is sleeping. We can talk more after you travel again."

Nyssa recognized the voice that had been calling to her outside. As if this woman's words caused it, the switch came over Nyssa again. She stood in the same cave, lighter this time and no sign of the sleeping girl. Instead of one woman in a red dress, she now saw six tiny women, each in a different color dress. She also noticed something else. These women had magnificently patterned butterfly wings.

"What happened to the girl?" asked Nyssa.

The one in the red said, "My dear, that was many years ago. Those sisters have gone on to do other things. My name is Ruby and these are my sisters. We've been waiting for you."

Ruby introduced each of her brightly colored sisters. The perfectly proportioned, yet miniature, women amazed Nyssa. She tried to remember their names: red Ruby, orange Coral, yellow Saffron, green Beryl, blue Ultramarine and purple Lilac.

"We are sometimes called the Prismata and this cave has been our home for many years. It has been such since the Passing Queen and will remain so until the Last Queen," Ruby paused. She looked like she remembered something so utterly sad. Then she finished with a comforting smile, "You will be safe here until you are ready to continue your journey."

Nyssa had so many questions and she was so tired. The first question came easy enough. She pointed at the pillows and cushions.

"May I sit there?" Nyssa asked.

"Of course," said Saffron. She fluttered to the side, clearing a path for Nyssa. All of the Prismata giggled as Nyssa plopped into the extremely comfortable seat.

Now, Nyssa took an opportunity to admire her surroundings. Although they were in a cave, the Prismata made it quite charming. They had plenty of shelves carved into the stone walls. Nyssa could not understand why, because every shelf was empty. They also had miniature stone chairs, one for each sister and each the exact right size for their small bodies.

Looking to the front of the cave, Nyssa did not realize how close they were to the entrance. She thought she walked much further in, but apparently not. The waterfall remained parted in the same way as when she first entered into the cave. From her soft spot, she could see most of the lagoon.

Instead of floating rocks, out on the center of the shimmering pool Nyssa saw one of the biggest, ugliest ducks she had ever seen. The thing had ruffled and torn feathers of mostly black and brown. It also had some dirt or grime encrusted around its beak. From her distance, she could not tell what the creature had been eating to cause that.

"That's gross," said Nyssa.

"What?" asked Beryl. She pointed to the lagoon. "Why that poor thing is only a duckling. It has many more years to grow."

Ruby blocked Nyssa's view. She said, "It is not unlike you. You stumbled into Empyrean, looking strange and unsure. Imagine what you might become once you complete your journey. Inside, you have tremendous beauty and potential, but you must give it a chance to grow. You had too many ugly things in your life. You have the chance to let that fall away as a duckling might lose its baby feathers and transform into something greater than before."

When Ruby finished, she moved and Nyssa could not believe it. The ugly duckling had turned into an immensely glorious swan. She knew it had to be the same creature because as it stretched its white wings, the last of the black feathers drifted up into the air. The swan craned its neck upward and let out a melodious, trumpet-like call. A moment later, it flapped its wings proudly and flew out of sight.

Nyssa stared at the calm surface of the lagoon. The swan did not leave a single ripple. In her own past, Nyssa wished many times that she could fly away like a bird. She never imagined herself as beautiful as a swan though. In fact, she could not recall anyone ever calling her beautiful, or even pretty.

It did not matter, she told herself. Nyssa always thought she was pretty. These Prismata said she could transform into someone beautiful. She liked that idea.

"Before you become lost in your thoughts," interrupted Ruby, "know that beauty is not only measured in your face. True beauty comes from your heart and your mind. It shines outward from your actions."

Lilac added, "Your actions and the decisions you make will affect how others see you. Keeping to yourself and avoiding others will make you easy to ignore. You will only transform if *you* want to."

"Okay. I get it," said Nyssa. She pulled her knees up to her chest, rested a pillow on them and let her head drop. Burying her face in the pillow did not make the vision of the swan leave her mind.

"No, you do not *get it* quite yet, but I think you will," said Ruby.

The sound of rushing water told Nyssa the waterfall draped closed again. She looked up quickly to confirm this and it had. Nyssa also expected the Prismata to be staring at her, but they were not. They seemed to busy themselves with their own conversation.

She wanted more of their attention and asked, "You said this was your home since the time of the Flashing Queen?"

Ultramarine chuckled. She said, "No dear. Not the Flashing Queen. The Passing Queen."

"Where did you live before here?" asked Nyssa.

Ruby rose from her stone chair and said, "By the will of the Deep Magic, we graced the sky from west to east to celebrate the deeds of the First Queen for one thousand years."

Coral said, "We descended to aid the Passing Queen forever giving up that home."

"That's amazing," said Nyssa. She did not really feel like she had any better words for it. She understood that they made a great sacrifice and did not know if she could ever do anything like that. She decided to change the subject.

"I have a problem," she said.

"Yes," said Ruby. "The Deep Magic has chosen you as a vessel, but your body is having difficulty absorbing it."

"Odin said I got some evil energy. He said it will run out soon though," explained Nyssa.

Saffron said, "That is somewhat correct. The Forgotten Evil is only one side of the same coin, if you take my meaning. The Deep Magic will only act according to your heart. Once it has chosen you though, I do not expect it will ever leave you."

"My sister is right," said Ruby. "You have been chosen for a purpose."

"What purpose?" demanded Nyssa. "Odin said all I have to do is get back to the start and this weird dream will be over."

Ruby fluttered close to Nyssa. She ran her tiny hand through the girl's wavy hair.

She said, "Your purpose is for you to discover. If we tell you what happens when you get there, then the journey will mean nothing. You must go back to the place where you first set foot in Empyrean. The path will be long and you will leave your impression across many times. There will come a time when *this dream* will seem like a nightmare."

Nyssa did not like the way Ruby talked to her. She made it seem like some bad things were going to happen.

"I think I want to go home," said Nyssa.

"Home is a place where you are safe and loved. Do you have a place like that?" asked Beryl.

This question hurt. Nyssa knew she had not had a real home in a long time. She also knew, so far, that this crazy world was far better than anything she had to go back to.

"No," Nyssa finally answered.

"Then you have to make your home here," said Ruby. "Open your heart and be willing to accept help from unlikely places. When you get to the end of your travels, you will be at the beginning."

This sounded like a riddle to Nyssa. She never was good at riddles and definitely did not feel like trying to figure it out right now. Instead, she had one other question. Nyssa pulled the three crystals from her pockets.

"Do you know what these are?" she asked.

Ruby gave a one word answer, "No."

The look on the red fairy's face made Nyssa think otherwise. She expected another riddle or some vague directions. She noticed that none of the other sisters would look at her. She felt like they were hiding something.

"I watched a woman get trapped inside these by a bad man. I hoped maybe you could help her," said Nyssa.

"If you come across any elves on your journey, ask them. That is all I can say," finished Ruby.

"Maybe this will help?" offered Ultramarine. She held up a pouch with a soft leather shoulder strap. She said, "It doesn't have a bottom. You can put anything in here, like those crystals, and never worry about filling it up."

Nyssa could not see anything inside the pouch. She stuck in her arm to gently set the crystals down, but she could not feel the bottom. Nyssa let go of the crystals and quickly looked in again. Still nothing. She reached in, only a short way, and pulled out one of the crystals. Satisfied that it would be safe, Nyssa put the crystal back in the pouch.

Ultramarine said, "All you have to do is think about something inside and it will be at your fingertips."

Ruby fluttered toward the cave entrance. She gestured for Nyssa to follow.

"It is time for you to be on your way. Do not take the direct path. You will find the right way by making some wrong choices. It is only mid-day and you can make it quite a way before dark. Farewell."

Coral called from the darkness of the cave, "Remember to open your heart."

The waterfall did not part this time. Nyssa left the Prismata and walked along the south edge of the lagoon. A noise echoed across the water. Nyssa looked up to see the beautiful swan one last time as it vanished in the blur of another switch.

Chapter 10

The First Song

In this forest, Nyssa could not see the sun above the treetops. She had no idea which way she was going. She tried to go in as straight of a line as she could manage. The thick underbrush and tight clusters of lush trees caused her to constantly redirect her course. The Prismata told her not to take a direct path anyway, so she did not let it frustrate her too much.

As she walked along, she could feel evening approaching. Nyssa did not need to see the sky to tell her it was getting dark.

The dimming light and complete silence of the forest made Nyssa feel quite alone. She expected, at least, to hear the chirping of a bird or some other animal chittering. No sound came to her.

This made her realize something else. She had no music. Over the past two days, Nyssa had not heard or thought about a single song, except for those villagers chanting by their fire. She remembered how the sound of the Banookanookans blended with the ocean. She wanted to make music like that. She wanted to make a beautiful, perfect song.

Nyssa did not feel the right emotions for that now. At present, she felt completely alone and a little frustrated at her slow progress. She concentrated on the fact that some of her favorite songs were about being alone. She believed the ones she wrote about her own loneliness were some of her best work. She tried to remember those lyrics to help pass the time.

Nothing came to her.

She could not remember any of her songs. Worse still, she guessed her notebook probably burned along with all of her other possessions in the fire at her foster parents' house.

As the forest grew darker, so did Nyssa's loneliness. It started somewhat to turn into fear. She did not like the idea of being in these strange woods by herself at night.

Suddenly, a clicking sound took her attention away from the impending dread. Something somewhere made a noise that disturbed the quiet of the woods, because it was not a sound of the woods. This thing seemed to be coming closer. Nyssa guessed by the sound that it was something small and metallic. The click sounded nothing like Shaydaway's rattling, clinking wagon.

Nyssa stepped into a small clearing, only wide enough to see the last of the fading sunlight. In a few steps, she could easily be back in the thick of the forest.

From here, Nyssa could clearly see the sky. With a lack of clouds, even in the fading light, she spotted the edge of a radiant rainbow.

This made Nyssa think of the Prismata. They said they once graced the sky. Maybe, Nyssa wondered, the rainbow sisters were the rainbow itself. That seemed a pleasant enough idea. From this, she also guessed that meant she had gone back in time. She had no idea how far back, but she thought the rainbow could be a good indicator for the next time. She hope she remembered to check the sky after each switch. Then, judging from the rainbow, she could tell if she had gone further into the past or back to the future.

Unexpectedly, the clicking noise came into the clearing, bringing her attention back to the present. The sound came from a small bird-like device that circled her head once before landing on a nearby branch. Nyssa immediately knew it was not a real bird by its shiny metallic *feathers*. Upon closer inspection, when it did not move, she could see tiny gears in its open neck and under its wing hinges. Despite being completely mechanical, it did remind her of a real type of bird from back home.

A nightingale.

Nyssa loved nightingales. She never saw one in real life. However, an old drama teacher once told her she sang like a nightingale. Since then, it became her favorite bird. She even cut pictures out of magazines and hung them on her wall. Of course, those would be ash now too.

"You are a curious thing," Nyssa said to the mechanical bird. She reached out to touch it.

The nightingale shrieked and flew up into the sky.

"Wait. Come back. I didn't mean to frighten you," said Nyssa. Even if it was only a bird, she did not want to be alone any longer.

The nightingale seemed to respond to her plea. Could it understand her, Nyssa wondered. The mechanical bird drifted back down to her. This time, it chose to land on her still outstretched finger.

"That's better," said Nyssa. "I could use a friend right now."

The nightingale gave a sympathetic coo.

Nyssa studied the little creation. Whoever put this mechanical bird together must have taken great pride in their work. The detail of its body amazed her, from the shine of its eyes to the rows of thin grooved metal covering its wings like layers of feathers. They were probably made of tin, she guessed.

"Where did you come from?" she asked.

The nightingale twisted its head completely backwards. Nyssa suspected its beak now pointed directly west. She found it interesting that the bird might have come from the direction she was supposed to be going.

"Your home is that way? Are you lost?"

Suddenly, the bird's head spun out of control. It made frantic whirring and chirping noises as it wildly flapped its wings, without rising into the air. Small puffs of steam shot out of a few different joints.

"You poor thing," Nyssa said. "I'm lost too."

The flashes of steam answered Nyssa's next question. She had not seen anything in this world to make her think they had electricity. This gizmo had to be steam powered, she deduced.

Nyssa felt sorry for the little bird. They both found themselves in similar situations. This instantly gave them a connection. At least, Nyssa hoped so.

She asked, "Would you like a new friend? Maybe I could help you find your way home?"

The bird responded with a new sound, like a royal trumpet in celebration. Apparently, this nightingale could do more than chirp. Then it opened its beak wider and an eruption of applause filled the night air. It seemed to be accepting Nyssa's offer. The overly positive response made Nyssa smile.

"You are a funny little thing," she said.

Wha, wha, wha came the horn-like sound of a stage comedian. The nightingale must have no limit to the sound effects it could make, Nyssa surmised.

"Maybe this will be a good place to sleep for the night," suggested Nyssa.

A bobbing head movement told Nyssa that the nightingale agreed. It flew from her hand to a low branch while Nyssa made herself comfortable. Staring up at the nightingale in the darkness, she could make out a faint blue glow.

"Oh, you have a night light too," said Nyssa.

With a couple of internal clicks, the blue light grew brighter and shone out of the nightingale's eyes. It cast a very pleasant aura wherever it looked, but mostly stayed focused on Nyssa.

She felt safe for the moment and tried to rest. Apparently, the nightingale wanted to sing her a lullaby. It started out simply sounding like a bird whistling, but after the first few bars, transformed into an imitation of a string quartet.

The beautiful music inspired Nyssa. Her new friend spoke to her in a language which she could understand. It awakened something in her that had been missing in this mysterious new world. On this dark and lonely night, haunting lyrics seemed to spill out of Nyssa's heart.

Now I lay me down to sleep,
In these woods so dark and deep,
With only you my special friend,
Until this song comes to an end.

Waiting for the sun to rise,
I sleep by the light of your bright eyes,
Carried on this tune you lend,
Until your song comes to an end.

Alone again, and yet no more.
My home was lost beyond the shore.
I'll be strong with the love you send,
Until my nightingale's song does end.

Chapter 11

The First Friend

When morning came, Nyssa awoke peacefully. The peace vanished suddenly. She did not see the nightingale anywhere. She must have switched in her sleep, she worried.

A brief glance at the bright morning sky displayed the shimmering rainbow to Nyssa.

"At least I'm still in the past," she said to no one.

Nyssa instantly developed an attachment to the mechanical nightingale and already missed her late night visitor.

Then a chirping noise came from behind her. The nightingale swooped in low. It carried a beautiful yellow flower. Nyssa raised her hands on instinct and the nightingale dropped the flower into her cupped palms. She smelled the delicate, curled petals that resembled a rose. The sweet scent almost made her sneeze. Nyssa gently pushed the stem behind her ear. Without a mirror, she could only imagine how the exotic flower looked surrounded by her wavy hair.

The nightingale let out a long whistle as Nyssa presented herself.

"Thank you," she said, thinking the nightingale complimented her flower. "I thought I lost you this morning."

As soon as she said this, Nyssa's vision started to blur. She did not want it to happen, but she switched and definitely lost her nightingale this time.

Not only did she lose the bird, but the rainbow did not grace the gloomy sky that somehow felt lower over her head. The entire forest seemed emptier, lonelier.

"It's not fair," Nyssa demanded.

Something caught Nyssa's attention from the corner of her eye. She turned, but the yellow glare stayed out of view. It took a moment for her to realize that she still had the flower tucked behind her ear. She pulled the yellow flower into view and wondered how it came with her from the past. She assumed that she must be able to bring things with her as long as she touched them. Thinking now, it made sense because her clothes and the Prismatas' pouch came with her just as those crystals had. What would happen if she grabbed a person or animal, she wondered.

If only she held the nightingale.

A snapping branch broke into Nyssa's lamentation.

Nyssa scanned the woods. The forest that made her lonely and uncomfortable last night, now gave her chills resulting in goose bumps on her arms. Everything felt lifeless despite the green growth of trees and the occasional palm. Nyssa decided nothing would live in a place like this.

Another broken twig told her she was wrong.

Somewhere outside of her view, something encircled her and it wanted to stay hidden. A moment ago, Nyssa would have wished to never switch again. Now, she could think of nothing except switching away from whatever approached. Nyssa did not want to meet any creature that called this place home.

She did not like the unnatural silence that perforated the snapping twigs. Then the crunch of dry leaves drew Nyssa's attention. She turned in time to spot a white rabbit at the edge of her small clearing. The large curve of its back haunches made the fur look more like a comfortable pillow. It stared at her with its reflective golden eyes and then hopped behind the closest tree. Nyssa dashed over to follow the rabbit like the character in one of her favorite books. Around the tree, she did not find the rabbit or even a hole. It had simply disappeared.

Nyssa did not like this whole situation.

She now started to worry that some bad magic might be coming for her, trying to capture her or permanently stop her. She could not believe such a large rabbit could suddenly vanish. There had to be a hole reasoned Nyssa. Then something rustled under an old dry leaf. A tiny white mouse, equally as furry as the rabbit, crawled out and sniffed the air. Nyssa spied tiny gold eyes on its pointy face.

"How strange," she said aloud about the peculiar coincidence. She had not seen too many animals and suspected they all might have golden eyes.

The mouse skittered across the damp soil, heading toward the small clearing where Nyssa spent the previous night. As it crossed the short distance, Nyssa watched the mouse transform into a hamster and then cat. Each animal shared the same silky white coat. The transition from one shape to the next tickled Nyssa as a short tail suddenly became a long one.

The cat stopped in the glade to stretch and roll in a warm sliver of sunlight fighting through the morning clouds. Nyssa's trepidation turned to amusement as she watched from a safe distance. The cat changed again. It grew instantly to the size of a horse and then shrunk to a pig. Each time, the hair and skin stayed white and the eyes shone gold. Nyssa wanted to go to the adorable piglet, but she hesitated. She thought she saw a third shape as the horse morphed into the pig. She thought she saw a human girl.

This confused Nyssa. She wondered if the creature might be dangerous. If she got too close, would the same thing happen to her, she considered. Stepping halfway into the clearing, the pig began snorting at Nyssa. It continued to snort as it transformed from the pig into the girl Nyssa thought she glimpsed a moment ago.

With the transformation, the grunting sound turned into words, "Snok...what are you looking at?"

Nyssa asked herself the same question.

How could she be staring at a girl that had only a moment ago been a little pig? This girl had white, shoulder-length hair and those same peculiar golden eyes. She had no pupils, only those gold disks floating in the white of her eyes. Nyssa thought her simple white dress looked comfortable enough. Her muddy bare feet made Nyssa wish for a bath herself. If only, she thought, there was a hotel near here. The girl looked young. Nyssa guessed maybe no more than ten or twelve years old. She must be terrified out her by her lonesome, Nyssa thought, since she felt the same.

Finally, Nyssa answered the girl, "I'm not sure. Were you a pig a second ago?"

The girl looked angry, probably as much from the question as the situation. She said, "Probably. I can't keep track. Some of the time, I can't even control it."

"Can you turn into any animal?" asked Nyssa, moving closer to the apparently friendly girl.

"So far. Why? Do you have a request?" responded the girl. She blinked her gold eyes and made a face that said Nyssa started to annoy her.

Nyssa felt embarrassed for being rude. She said, "No. I'm sorry. Can you tell me your name?"

The girl looked surprised by the question, then she smiled. Looking more relaxed, she said, "I'm Aleria."

Nyssa loved the sound of her new friend's name. Although Aleria was a few years younger, she thought they might easily become good friends. That thought caused her to flash back to how she lost the nightingale. She met Aleria by chance, but would hate to lose her in the same way. She did not want to get too emotionally close, but wanted to know more about this girl.

"What happened to you?" asked Nyssa.

Aleria looked at herself like she did not know what Nyssa meant. Then with a look of realization, she said, "Oh, you mean the changy-thing. It's a curse, kind of. My mom sent me to Baba Yaga for a protection charm against the dwarves. I'm pretty sure the old hag planned to eat me instead, but I got away. She did hit me with this curse when she couldn't chase me anymore."

"That sounds terrible," said Nyssa.

"It gets worse," said Aleria. She leaned casually against a tree, which made her story less frightening. "When I finally made it home, my mama was gone and the whole village was deserted. Since then, I've been on my own. At least the curse has kept me safe from the dwarves. When they pop up, they are only interested in human kids, not cute, cuddly animals."

Nyssa said, "What a horrible story. I'm so sorry." She felt a growing connection. "I thought I saw some dwarves carrying a baby."

"That sounds like them. I've seen their destruction all over the east. My village used to be on the other side of the wasteland," said Aleria.

"Is that to the west?" asked Nyssa. "I'm heading west."

Aleria looked over her shoulder, as if someone might be following her. Nyssa did not like that, but she liked the girl's words even less. Aleria said, "Yes. It's pretty dangerous, but I can show you a fairly safe way to cross it."

This idea excited Nyssa. Finally, she had someone willing to help her on her journey. She would have both a friend and a guide. Then her vision started to blur. Nyssa could feel the switch coming over her.

"Grab my hand," shouted Nyssa, as she reached for Aleria. She saw the younger girl reach for her with a surprised look an instant before she switched. She knew they were too late.

Once she regained her vision, Nyssa surveyed her surroundings. The forest looked full of life, not nearly as dreadful. Aleria had mentioned the dwarves causing some destruction, so Nyssa guessed she went back in time before that started. However, she saw no sign of the Prismata rainbow. She must not have gone back too far, she surmised.

She truly began to dislike the switching. Like the nightingale, she could not find Aleria now either. She guessed the girl did not reach her in time, or maybe other living things could switch with her. Nyssa had gained and lost two friends in less than a day and this saddened her.

A tickling sensation on her forearm stopped Nyssa from feeling sorry for herself. She twisted her arm upward, trying to look at the back of her elbow. The odd sensation moved from her hand in that direction. Clinging to the underside of her arm, Nyssa discovered a fuzzy white caterpillar.

The caterpillar dropped from Nyssa's arm before it reached her elbow. In midair, it turned into a butterfly without the need for a cocoon. The butterfly hovered for a moment in front of Nyssa before it became Aleria again.

"What was that?" asked a still surprised looking Aleria.

"Uh," was all Nyssa could bolster. Then she said, "I guess I kind of have a curse too. As best as I understand it, I can time travel. I don't really have any control over my problem either."

Aleria looked at her new surroundings. She rubbed the bark of the trees and sniffed a bunch of unusual orange flowers. She briefly turned into a dog and rolled on the soft grass. Then she changed back into a girl.

"We're in the past," offered Nyssa.

"We have to be," agreed Aleria. "I've only ever heard stories of the forest looking like this. Some of these plants are extinct in my time."

Aleria looked like she loved it and that made Nyssa happy. It also made her happy that she was able to stay with her new friend despite the switch. Then she realized that she took Aleria from her own time with no definite way back.

Nyssa blurted, "I'm sorry I took you away from your mom and your village. I didn't want to be alone, but I should have told you first."

Aleria looked Nyssa in the face. She said, "I told you my family was gone. I had almost no chance of finding them. I've been cursed for two years. Don't be sorry. There's nothing you could have done."

"You're not mad?" asked Nyssa.

"Nope," said Aleria. She apparently could not stop smelling flowers and scrunching her toes in the thick grass. "I offered to help you go west. If we get separated, how can I do that? Besides, I've been getting better at controlling my problem. Maybe I can help you with yours?"

Nyssa liked the idea of having Aleria as a companion. In a way, it felt like she had a kid sister. Nyssa thought how strange it would be to have to travel to another world in order to find a family.

"Okay," Nyssa said. "Stay close. When the switch starts, I'll probably only have a few seconds to warn you. If we're not touching, then I'll switch without you."

"That's an easy solution," Aleria said. She slipped her pale, slightly smaller hand into Nyssa's and led her into the forest.

Chapter 12

The First Messenger

The girls strolled through the woods almost as if they were looking for a good spot to have a picnic lunch. In this mood, Nyssa let a lot of her worries slip from her mind. She did not feel any urgency or danger.

Aleria looked happy, as well. Nyssa studied the girl while she studied their surroundings. This unusual new friend seemed to be in tune with nature. Birds and flowers responded to her. As she came near, flowers would lean towards her and birds would flutter in the lower branches. Mostly, they appeared to be hummingbirds. Nyssa saw no sign of her nightingale. Like any problems that troubled Empyrean, she thought the nightingale must be a million miles, or years, from them.

Then, like a reminder of where she was and what she had to do, the switch came over her. The blurring passed and Nyssa wanted to make sure Aleria was still with her.

"What an unusual sensation," said Aleria. They held each other's hand the same as they did before the switch. Aleria used her other hand and patted the top of her head, apparently checking on the condition of her hair. "It feels different in human form."

"What do you mean?" asked Nyssa.

"I'm not sure. Maybe blurrier? Do you know what I mean?" said Aleria.

Nyssa did know what she meant. With every switch, her vision blurred almost to the point of causing pain. More importantly, Nyssa wanted to know *when* they were. The surrounding forest did not look any different. However, an intense rainbow cut a path across the sky.

"We've gone further back," deduced Nyssa. Having sight of the Prismata in their rainbow form made the switch slightly more tolerable.

"This is wonderful," said Aleria.

The younger girl looked impressed with their new surroundings, although nothing seemed different to Nyssa.

Aleria continued, "From the looks of things, we shouldn't have to go much further north."

"North?" Nyssa did not like the sound of that. She said, "We're supposed to be going west. Why would you lead us north?" Nyssa let her hand drop from Aleria's. They stood apart for the first time since leaving that little clearing.

Aleria looked at Nyssa. She rolled her eyes ever so slightly, the gold reflected the sun. She explained, "The Great Road is the fastest way to get to the mountains."

A flash of anger and panic momentarily ran over Nyssa. She composed herself, grabbed Aleria's hands into her own and said, "That is where I saw the dwarves and that wicked carnival man."

"Well, I don't know anything about this carnival man, but we shouldn't have to worry about any dwarves if we've gone back as far as you say. As long as the Royal Forest is green throughout, we should be safe," said Aleria.

"What does that have to do with it?" asked Nyssa.

"A green forest is a living forest," said Aleria. "It means that the dwarves have not started mining and killing the land."

That made sense to Nyssa. She silently conceded that Aleria knew the forest better than her. Still, it made her nervous to head back to that open road. She did not want Aleria to end up like Kisa and decided to tell her that story.

Close to the end of the story, a new voice interrupted them causing both girls to jump. They hurriedly looked around for whoever called out to them.

"Up here," he said.

The girls spun around and looked up the trunk of the closest tree. On the lowest branch, Nyssa spotted a small, brown squirrel and no one or nothing else.

"Are you talking to us?" she asked.

"I don't expect there is anyone else around," said the squirrel.

As if in response to the statement, Aleria suddenly, and possibly unintentionally, turned into a white squirrel. Almost as suddenly, she popped back into her human form.

Looking slightly distracted, the squirrel said, "My name's Rata and I've been looking for you."

"How could you have possibly been looking for us?" Aleria said defensively. "We only got her a minute ago."

Rata jumped from the safety of his high perch to a lower, closer branch. He looked to be considering Aleria's words. He said, "From your perspective, I guess that is true. From my perspective, I've been waiting for you for three years."

This shocked Nyssa. She knew she had only been here a few days. She now realized that pieces of those days must span several hundred years. When Rata announced who was looking for her, it shocked her even more.

Rata said, "I've been commissioned by a nightingale to deliver a message."

"You saw my nightingale?" Nyssa almost shouted. "Where is he?"

Nyssa's surprised reaction caused Rata to instinctively bolt backward. He scurried around the tree trunk and cautiously peeked out from his safe spot.

She did not want to frighten the squirrel any more, but Nyssa had too many questions. "Where did you see him? What is his message? How could you understand him?"

Rata seemed to settle. He said, "First, please maintain some self-control. If you cannot control what is within, then everything without will always be chaos."

"I'm sorry," said Nyssa. She realized she was acting a little wild. Rata's words made sense, though. She tried to calm herself. In her defense, she said, "I lost him so suddenly."

Rata climbed down to the ground and stopped at Nyssa's feet. She squatted to hear him better.

"That is understandable. To answer some of your questions, as a messenger, I have a duty to learn all of the languages of Empyrean. There are many. Your friend's speech is a unique sound in the east, but much more common in the west. It did not take me long to learn it."

"There are more nightingales?" Nyssa asked excitedly.

Rata said, "No. No more nightingales, but many more of his mechanical kind."

Nyssa's imagination ran away with her. What other steam-powered creatures could live in the west, she wondered. She wished she could see a land populated with mechanical animals, but somehow she knew she never would. The west that Rata spoke of had to be on the other side of her destination. Even if she did go far west, she had no guarantee that she would arrive in the correct time. She decided to focus on her task.

"When you last saw your friend," Rata continued, "he was attempting to guide you along your path. He knew you were lost."

"But I thought he was the one that was lost," said Nyssa. She thought she was trying to help the poor little thing, alone in the woods. She could not believe he was trying to help her.

"I presume you have not experienced it yet in your time line, but the nightingale told me he met you years before your encounter in the woods," said Rata.

"That doesn't seem possible," Aleria started. Then she said, "I mean, that's not possible for normal people. I don't think either of us is normal. I know you are special."

Nyssa smiled at the idea of not being normal, but then she lost track of the conversation. In her old life, no one would have ever called her *special*. She never felt important or different. Now she knew she was all of those. Aleria's simple compliment warmed Nyssa's heart. She did not mind being different because different meant she was special.

The messenger squirrel looked annoyed. He cleared his throat loudly and said, "If I may deliver the message, I can be on my way and leave you to yours. There are others that require my services."

"Our apologies," said Aleria. She gave an exaggerated bow.

Rata gave Aleria a sideways glance, then shrugged off her behavior. He said, "The message is: friend Nightingale wants you to know he will be there when you need him most, but you will have to set him free in order that he may set you free."

The message made almost no sense to Nyssa. She wanted an explanation from Rata, but he darted back up into the trees and out of sight. He did his duty and left them alone.

"What kind of message was that?" asked Aleria. Apparently, she did not understand it either.

"I don't know," said Nyssa. "It sounds like we will be meeting the nightingale again. I like that idea."

Aleria smiled. Then she turned into a dog. She walked in a small circle, sniffing the ground and the air. After a moment, she changed back and said, "Come on, there should be a place not too far from here that I want you to see. I wonder what it looked like before it was frozen?"

Chapter 13

The First Romance

Nyssa enjoyed the woods. Without giants at war or someone trying to kidnap her, everything looked beautiful. She felt like it could stir her heart to music. However, the sounds of birds and the occasional growling animal drowned out anything inside her.

On this walk, Aleria went back to holding Nyssa's hand. They continued on a fairly wide path that seemed to lead directly north. This made Nyssa a little nervous, not knowing what awaited them in that direction. Having Aleria with her gave Nyssa a sense of security though.

For once, she did not feel totally alone.

She felt even better that the strange girl could switch with her. As long as they touched, they shared the experience. When they switched to a sky with no rainbow, Nyssa knew they went forward in time.

"I hope we didn't go too far forward," said Aleria. "In my time, there is a grove covered in ice. It is unbelievable."

Nyssa looked overhead at the thick, full trees. She said, "How long had this forest been dead in your time?"

Aleria looked surprised. She spun around, taking in the continuous amounts of green. She suddenly turned into a white raccoon with a gold mask and scampered into the bushes. A moment later, she turned human and popped up out of the underbrush. A twig caught in her white hair, but it did not seem to bother her. She held out a handful of brightly colored flowers.

"You're right," Aleria said. "I didn't notice how wonderful this place is. In my time, you couldn't find a single flower in all of the Dead Forest. You had to go past the frozen grove to even seen anything green. How long was this forest dead? They say it started at least fifty years before I was born."

Nyssa used her basic math skills and some simple deduction. She said, "That means we are at least fifty years before you were born, but sometime after the Passing Queen."

Nyssa apparently surprised Aleria again. A peculiar look splashed across the girl's face as she climbed out of the bushes.

"How do you know about the Passing Queen?" asked Aleria. She mumbled the next part, but Nyssa thought she heard, "It couldn't be her."

Nyssa wondered if that meant Aleria thought she might become the Passing Queen. She could not imagine herself as a queen and did not believe it could ever happen. She pushed the unthinkable out of her head. Instead, she said, "The Prismata told me about her."

Aleria's surprise turned to laughter. She giggled uncontrollably until she fell to the ground with great belly laughs. She transformed into a duck and the laughs transformed into quacks, but they did not slow. QUACK, QUACK, QUACK. Nyssa liked Aleria, but she did not like being laughed at.

The little white duck finally got herself under control. That control led to her changing back into Aleria. It did not stop her from smiling or eeking out a random giggle. She looked to be fighting her amusement as she said, "You met the *Prismata*?"

"Yes." Nyssa did not see anything funny. She liked the Prismata. Although they looked different, she did not think that was a laughing matter. Being different should not earn teasing from anybody.

Stifling another laughing fit, Aleria said, "The Prismata is a baby story. They're not real."

The accusation stung, coming from her new friend. "They are real," stated Nyssa. "They gave me this bottomless pouch." She held up the cloth bag as evidence.

"Everybody has bottomless pouches. Baba Yaga has at least three. I think somebody tried to con you," said Aleria.

This frustrated Nyssa. She said, "You say everybody has one of these bags, we met a talking squirrel, and you have a curse, but you don't believe in the Prismata?"

Aleria's mood shifted to seriousness. She looked almost indignant. She said, "I don't believe in Father Odin either, but I still got a present on Queen's Day every year until..."

She trailed off to a melancholy silence. Nyssa thought she saw a tear at the corner of the girl's golden eye.

"Hey, I'm sorry," said Nyssa. She guessed the mention of Queen's Day caused her to think about her mom. Nyssa did not know how long Aleria had been on her own. She did know the heartbreak of losing her parents though. They had that in common and Nyssa thought it might create a strong bond. She threw her arm around Aleria's shoulder and said, "Come on."

Aleria started to move again. She sniffled, holding back those tears, and said, "Next, I suppose you are going to tell me you saw a dragon?"

Nyssa recalled seeing a dragon when she first arrived in Empyrean as she sailed over that village. She decided not to answer Aleria's question. Apparently, dragons were also considered make believe and Nyssa did not want to start another argument.

The girls walked on quietly, until the path veered to the left. A short way into the woods on the right, Nyssa could see the ground slope up along a wide curve.

"This is the place. It looks a little different, but I'm sure it is," said Aleria. She tugged at Nyssa as she darted up into the woods.

At the top of the small rise, they stopped. Nyssa looked down into a clearing ringed with narrow trees. The ring of trees looked too perfect to be accidental. She guessed someone must have planted them to surround the clearing. Except, it was more than a clearing. Stunning flowers of every variety made it an exquisite garden.

Nyssa had never seen flowers like these. Some had many tiny petals. Others had large petals, like wings swaying in the breeze. Bright colors competed to outdo each other. Even the ones that looked like black roses seemed perfectly at home among the reds, yellows, pinks and purples. White boughs with small orange-like fruits hung from some of the trees. Nyssa thought she could smell their sweet scent and wondered how they tasted.

A dark brown stone stuck out of the ground at the far edge of the circular garden. From this distance, Nyssa could barely make out a trickle of water bubbling out of a crack on the top of the nearly rectangular stone. She could see the shimmer of water seeping down the sides of the stone. The fertile ground immediately absorbed it.

"It must be magic," whispered Nyssa. She could not bring herself to speak any louder in this beautiful setting.

"What?" asked Aleria.

Nyssa clarified, "The fountain must be magic, or at least the water. I bet the water is soaking the ground keeping these flowers young and fresh. I don't see a dry leaf anywhere inside the circle."

Aleria shrugged, as if she was not interested. Before she could add anything else, Nyssa heard voices coming from the far side of the garden. The girls ducked behind an untamed hedge as a young man and young woman came into view below them.

The man, well, almost a man, but still with enough boyish features to make Nyssa think he was cute, seemed upset. He pushed a thin branch out of his way with enough force to snap it from the tree as he stomped into the circle. The flowering petals on that broken branch instantly faded and withered. He did not seem to notice what he had done.

The cute, angry, young man with long brown hair hanging down over the shoulders of his tunic said, "Why does it have to be today?"

Until now, Nyssa could not clearly see the young woman's face. The recipient of the boy's angry question, barely older than Nyssa herself, stepped into the clearing. Nyssa recognized her despite her young appearance. It only took her a moment to remember where she last saw the raven-haired woman.

Remina.

Nyssa remembered Remina as the queen building the sand castle by the sea. After she lost Kisa to that wicked Raymond Shaydaway, she wanted to run to Remina for help. She thought now would be a good time to ask for help and started to move.

Before Nyssa could clear the bushes, Aleria grabbed her forearm and silently gestured for her to wait. Apparently, Aleria wanted to hear some of their conversation without revealing themselves. If the young couple was arguing, Nyssa agreed that it might be better to wait.

The somewhat younger version of Remina looked on the verge of tears. She maintained her composure as she said, "William, I am sorry. I am so sorry. You know I have no control over this."

Remina's consolations did not seem to make the cute boy named William any happier. He ran his left hand through his long hair. Then he let his hand drop to the hilt of the sword hanging from his belt. Nyssa did not think he was going to do anything senseless with the sword, but she guessed sometimes love made people unpredictable. She already assumed these two were in love. Something clearly came between them.

The glint of the jewel on the hilt of William's sword flashed a reflection of the afternoon sun in Nyssa's eyes. Nyssa squinted and when she looked back, William said, "I know it is not your doing, but why does it have to be on our wedding day?"

A wedding? Nyssa began to understand the situation. The way they dressed made more sense too. She looked at their clothes. William wore a tunic laced with gold trim. It really looked too nice for everyday wear, especially here in the forest. Remina's blue dress did not seem quite as nice as the simple white one she wore the first time Nyssa saw her on the beach. Still, it looked far more beautiful than any dress Nyssa ever wore. Nyssa remarked again that Remina looked younger than their last meeting. She deduced this had to be some time before the beach, sometime before the building of the sand castle.

"My dearest William, when the Queen of the Eastern Sky passes into the twilight, the new queen is called." Remina took both of William's hands in hers. It looked like a compassionate embrace to Nyssa. Remina continued, "You know the queen is not allowed to take a husband."

As the scene progressed, William seemed to calm a little. He also started to look a little defeated from what Nyssa could see.

"It doesn't make sense," said William. He plopped to the ground on his backside and pulled his knees up so he could rest his folded arms on them. Remina knelt beside him, her dress tucked under her legs.

She said, "Think on this. I have been chosen by the Deep Magic. I am to become a role model and symbol. My strength and independence will guide all of the citizens of the Eastern Sky and Empyrean. I make this sacrifice so that other young girls can live freely and enjoy life, in hopes that they will one day find a handsome young man to love and honor them as you do me. Every girl should learn to stand on her own first, so that her one true love will always respect her."

Nyssa loved that idea. She had been on her own most of her life, at least, that is how she felt. She did not think she was as strong as Remina. She wished she could be, though. She agreed that girls like her and Aleria needed to have role models like Remina.

"But I don't want to lose you," said William, with a tear in his eye. This caused Nyssa to back off of her idea a little. She barely knew Remina and did not know William at all. All the same, she hated to see them forced to separate.

Remina leaned next to William and now ran her fingers through his hair. It reminded Nyssa of a gesture that a mother might do to a child, but there was a different kind of affection in the movement. Remina said, "It is a sacrifice we will make together." She paused, seemingly considering something. A faint smile graced her lips as she said, "I have an idea. Stand up."

The fated couple stood at the same time.

"All right. Give me your sword and kneel," instructed Remina.

"But I..." started William. He looked confused, but followed the instructions. Nyssa guessed he must really trust Remina. The soon-to-be queen rested the flat edge of the blade on William's right shoulder. He looked at the sword and then up to Remina.

She said, "I know I am not yet officially queen, but here is my first proclamation. Honorable William of Fountainhead, I hereby decree you to be my squire and protector forever and always."

Apparently, William could no longer contain his tears. He cried, but he smiled at the same time. The sword dropped from Remina's hand and landed with a thud on the ground. William stood and hugged her intensely. Nyssa worried that he might crush Remina as hard as William looked to be squeezing her. Then the couple kissed. Nyssa did not know it would be their last kiss.

As she watched the couple, Nyssa felt her vision blur, signaling a coming switch. Nyssa wanted to talk to Queen Remina before she switched to another time, so she bolted from her hiding spot. In her haste, she did not grab Aleria's hand. She did not think about any of the consequences, except talking to Remina.

"Your Majesty, I need your help," Nyssa shouted across the small clearing.

The startled pair turned toward the two strange girls running out of the woods. Nyssa could feel Aleria tugging at her shirt, trying to keep her from interrupting the couple.

Then the blurring vision stopped. Nyssa did not switch.

Remina and William stood in front of her in the garden. Nothing changed. Everything looked the same. Aleria clamped down on Nyssa's shoulder. She looked to be catching her breath from the sudden excitement. Nyssa felt frozen. She expected to switch and then realized she would have lost Aleria by being selfish. Maybe Remina could answer her questions, but did she really want to lose Aleria because of it? Nyssa felt guilty and dropped her eyes. She saw Remina's bare toes sticking out beneath the hem of her wedding dress.

"It seems my responsibilities begin already," laughed Remina. She turned to William, "You see, I told you this was meant to be. I intend to be a beacon to young ladies everywhere." Remina turned back to Nyssa and finished with, "How can I help you?"

Nyssa did not get a chance to answer Remina's question. The switch that started a moment ago with blurry vision struck hard, hard enough to knock Nyssa back into Aleria. The girls stumbled backward. Nyssa's head hurt for a moment, like bumping into the edge of a door frame.

When Nyssa could see clearly again, she could not see Remina or William. Looking around, things seemed mostly the same outside of the garden. However, inside the ring of trees, ice covered everything. The bare branches no longer proudly bloomed. The flowers that previously covered the ground completely disappeared. At the far end of the garden, ice stretched from the tip of the fountain, down its bumpy, uneven sides, across the ground and up to a larger block of ice in the center of the clearing. Strangely, Nyssa did not feel cold.

"I don't think we're back in my time," said Aleria from behind her. "The ice stretched much further into the forest in my time."

Fortunately, the pain of the switch passed quickly so Nyssa could pay attention to her friend. She guessed it hit her harder because of the false start. She had no reason to know this for certain, but it seemed reasonable. She wondered if maybe the magic of this garden blocked it somehow, at least for a moment. Nyssa felt Aleria let go of her and she watched her friend peer into the large chunk of ice in the center of the frozen garden. Aleria put her hands up to the side of her face to get a better view.

"I think I see someone inside," said the white-haired girl.

"That's imposs..." started Nyssa. She could not finish her sentence as she tumbled to the ground. The slick ice stole her balance.

A giggle came from outside the circle. As Nyssa steadied herself she realized someone had to be watching them from outside the circle. Contrary to Nyssa's feelings, whoever watched thought Nyssa's fall was funny.

"Oh, did you like that?" Nyssa shouted from her hands and knees on the ground. She inched her way, crawling like a baby, to the edge of the garden and solid ground. Over her shoulder, she saw Aleria turn into a penguin and follow behind her.

When Nyssa could safely stand on the dry dirt, she looked up the short incline where she heard the giggle. A little girl, maybe five years old, sat watching them. Matted brown hair hung in her eyes and dirt stained her hands and shins. Her short dress, or possibly a long shirt, hung almost to her knees with a tattered hem. Whoever should be responsible for this ragamuffin of a child seemed to be failing in their duties.

"Why are you out here all alone?" asked Aleria, now back in human form. The shape shifting did not seem to frighten the little girl.

The waif said, "I'm not. I'm with my big brother."

Nyssa did not like the sound of that. She guessed this girl's brother to be equally as raggedy and possibly dangerous. If he did not care to keep his sister clean and safe, what did he care about, she wondered. Maybe he was some kind of criminal?

Aleria pressed, "Then where is your brother?"

The girl giggled again. She pointed into the frozen garden, toward the ice block, and said, "Right there."

Nyssa looked, but did not see anyone hiding behind the block of ice or near the icy fountain. She said, "I don't see anyone."

The girl stood up and pointed again, directly at the middle of the garden. She said, "He's right there. In the ice. He's stuck."

"What?" said Nyssa. Aleria must have been right.

As if she needed confirmation, Aleria added, "I told you someone was in there."

The little girl continued, ignoring Aleria's comment, "That's my brother. I'm his sister, Mia.

He was supposed to go away with some girl before I was born, but she never sent for him. Then he got stuck. My mom told me about it. She said he has a busted heart that turned him cold. I come visit him every day to see when he can get out."

Nyssa wanted to hug Mia. The girl's story made her sad, especially after seeing how much William and Remina were in love. Nyssa guessed that Remina left to be queen and never had the chance to come back for him. This made her think that a queen's life must be full of sacrifice and sadness. She could not ever imagine wanting that responsibility.

Mia started to leave them.

"Where are you going?" asked Nyssa. She did not want any little girl walking alone in these woods. With the iced over garden, Nyssa felt like something worse could be lingering near. The garden once felt full of life and magic, but now the surrounding forest seemed absolutely dreadful.

"I have to go home," said Mia. "Don't you?"

You have no idea, Nyssa wanted to say. Instead, Aleria spoke. "Where's your home?"

Mia pointed away from the circle, toward the path they saw earlier. She said, "I live in Frostwick. It's not far." She skipped down the hill.

"But I thought this place was called Fountainhead," said Nyssa.

"Not anymore," Mia called, without looking back at them. She kept skipping down the lonely path until Nyssa could no longer see her. Part of her wanted to follow Mia, but another part wanted to see if she could free William from the block of ice. She did not think he deserved that after losing his true love.

A slight headache flared, keeping Nyssa from doing either. She bent over and put her hands on her knees. The world started to swim. Aleria put a hand on Nyssa's back and that seemed to steady her a little.

"What's happening?" asked Aleria.

"The switches..." began Nyssa. Before she could finish her sentence, they switched. "...are starting to hurt," she finished.

This time, the pain flared out from the base of her skull. It rushed through her brain in a race to burst out of her eyes. Her eyes did not actually burst, but the pain pushed out with the blurred vision. For a moment, her head felt like an over-inflated balloon that might pop. The intense pain faded as rapidly as it came on, but it left her with an upset stomach.

Maybe, Nyssa thought, she needed to eat. It had been a while, but there looked to be little chance of that happening. The ice from the cursed garden now stretched far into the desolate forest.

Aleria said, "Feels like home to me."

Chapter 14

The First Stallion

Everything in Empyrean seemed so sad, thought Nyssa. She thought life in high school was depressing. With the Forgotten Evil threatening the land, everything seemed much worse. Everybody she met seemed to be heading toward some terrible end. So far, she met a queen who had to leave her prince on their wedding day, only for her castle to eventually fall to ruin. She met some wonderful fairies that had to give up their colorful grace in the sky. Even simple villagers, like Kisa and Aleria, found troubles in their lives.

Nyssa did not pretend to understand the balance the Atumval brought to the Forgotten Evil. She knew what Odin and Gilgamesh told her and she knew the Atumval was lost. As sad as Empyrean seemed, it held more promise and excitement than her old life. Nyssa contemplated never returning home. Part of her wanted to go back, but more of her heart wanted to remain.

If she decided to stay in Empyrean, she knew she did not want to live in a world constantly moving toward despair. She hoped there might be some other way to stop the Forgotten Evil without the Atumval. Maybe, Nyssa entertained, that she could somehow go back in time, to the beginning. If she could somehow control her switching, maybe she could go back to Odin and the others. Maybe she could help them stop this terrible thing.

In truth, she realized she was only a young girl who did not even have magic. She asked herself how she could possibly defeat the dark force known as the Forgotten Evil, let alone try to face it.

More than that, the last two times she switched, it started to hurt. It scared Nyssa to think what might happen the next time. What if the pain got worse? What if it lasted longer, she wondered. She did not want to think about really getting hurt. She encountered enough dangers that she did not want to be a danger to herself. The headache from the last switch faded after a few seconds, but the stomach ache lingered almost until they came to the edge of the Wasteland.

Nyssa and Aleria left the frozen part of the forest behind at Nyssa's insistent request. She wanted to keep moving now more than ever. If she could not control when the switches happened *or when* they would take her, she at least wanted to be moving in the right direction. Aleria did not seem to mind the frozen forest, but she said she wanted to stay with Nyssa.

Looking into the white expanse ahead of them, Aleria said, "This isn't going to be fun. It gets cold and windy at night and will probably take us a couple days to cross."

"You said you crossed it before. How did you make it?" asked Nyssa.

"Like this." Aleria instantly transformed into something that Nyssa thought looked like an armadillo. Like most things in Empyrean, it looked familiar, but was not quite the same. The similarity to an armadillo ended with the armored back. Aleria now had about twenty legs, no tail and was at least twice as big as any armadillo Nyssa had ever seen in a book or on TV.

Aleria changed back and said, "It's called a dirt bandit. I've never heard of one outside of the Central Plains, but this curse seems to know what I need before I need it. Last time, it happened on its own."

Nyssa looked out across the empty space. Gray and white sand greeted her without hope or comfort. She did not want to travel with Aleria in that animal form, but she did not think both of them should have to suffer the cold, windy nights.

"I still say it will be safer to go to the Great Road," offered Aleria, as if she could read Nyssa's thoughts.

"That's too far north," said Nyssa. She did not want to admit that she was scared of the dwarves that might be on that road. "We should go straight across. Remember, the Prismata told me to make my own path."

Aleria smiled at this, but did not start another argument about whether or not the fairies were real. This gave Nyssa pause to wonder if the Prismata meant a literal or figurative path. Aleria seemed to accept Nyssa's reason. She said, "Okay. Maybe we can get down in the trenches to stay out of the wind. Don't go jumping into the big cracks too fast though. Some of them don't have bottoms."

Despite the possible pitfalls, the girls did not have a very difficult time crossing the unpleasant terrain. Most of the time, they walked in silence. Aleria kept her human form. Nyssa started to pretend Aleria was a younger sister she never had in order to occupy her thoughts. She wished they were real sisters and not somebody's foster children. Then she realized she would never wish for anybody's sister to have to make a journey like this.

The entire time in the Wasteland, Nyssa did not switch once and that made her grateful. She did not like the randomness of it and definitely did not like the new headaches. All the same, the girls held hands as they walked. Better to not risk switching without Aleria, thought Nyssa. When they finally climbed up out of the last crevasse, the girls stood, shoulder-to-shoulder, in front of another expanse of the Dead Forest.

"Ugh," said Nyssa. "More good news."

"Hey, I was born here," said Aleria.

Nyssa could not tell if she was faking being insulted. She wanted to say *you might die here*. She decided that was too depressing of an idea, so she said, "Are you going to invite me in, then?"

This made Aleria laugh. She hugged Nyssa and then led the way into the Dead Forest.

As they walked, Aleria explained, "The Wasteland is like a rotten spot in the middle of the Dead Forest."

"The Dead Forest is like a rotten spot," added Nyssa.

"You're a rude guest, speaking so about my home," said Aleria. This time she seemed more like she was joking.

Both girls shared a laugh that ended abruptly. Nyssa became instantly aware of the frightfully quiet woods. Aleria must have sensed it too. Then a strange sound tore away the silence. A low rumbling came to them from deeper in the forest.

Aleria morphed into an owl and winged her way up to a high branch. She cocked her head and appeared to be listening intently. Waiting with concern, Nyssa guessed Aleria could hear far better in that form. A moment later, the beautiful white owl sailed down from the branch. She changed in mid-air and landed on human feet.

"It sounds like horses," Aleria said.

Nyssa immediately imagined them to be some evil, stampeding breed. She automatically expected every creature in this horrible place to be some type of villain.

Apparently Aleria did not feel the same as she said, "Let's go find them. Maybe we can get a ride."

Nyssa had not thought of that. She had been preparing herself for another escape. Walking almost non-stop for the past three days, her legs slipped past sore and right into numb. The idea of riding a horse anywhere seemed like a pleasant possibility. She hoped these animals would be friendly enough to allow them the chance to ride.

A short distance away, Aleria led them out of the Dead Forest and into a vibrant, fragrant meadow. Bright green grass covered the shallow rolling valley, with small patches of flowers dotting it here and there. Nyssa could not believe this hidden paradise existed in the middle of such a dreadful place. She could see that while the meadow was huge, icky, dead trees still surrounded it on all sides.

For the moment, that did not matter. The rhythmic pounding of hoof beats filled the air as the herd rounded the far side of the meadow. The timpani of hooves became deafening as the horses came close to them. Except, Nyssa discovered, they were not horses.

Unicorns.

Nyssa wanted to take back every bad thought she had about Empyrean and this awful Dead Forest. She loved unicorns since she was a little girl. They had always been a bright spot in her troubled life. From posters on her walls to school notebooks to a small decorative chest she once kept at the foot of her bed, unicorns decorated her life and existed in her imagination. She hoped, but never guessed they could be real.

Stunning white coats, like swirling clouds, rushed by with golden horns flashing and reflecting as bright as the sun. Nyssa had to put her hands over her ears, but she did not close her eyes as the herd came close and then continued to gallop along the edge of the meadow. She tried, but quickly gave up, counting. There had to be hundreds of them running in front of her.

As the noise of the main herd faded, a smaller herd of young unicorns struggled to keep up with the older ones. One of the young ones must have spotted Nyssa and Aleria. It veered over to them and stopped at the edge of the woods. The rest of the young herd followed and Nyssa suddenly found herself living a dream as she faced eight unicorns. She saw that they only had nubs where their horns should be and guessed they must be quite young.

"Fillies," said Aleria.

Nyssa did not have any experience with real horses, but she learned once that young females were called fillies. It seemed right that unicorns be only female. She did not expect to see any colts in this herd.

One of the unicorns, with eyes as blue as the ocean Nyssa touched only a few days before, came closest to Nyssa. She asked, "What are you doing here?"

Nyssa almost started to respond, but stopped short. She could not believe that a unicorn spoke to her. She barely allowed herself to believe they existed and now she discovered they could talk. Accepting all of that, she could not believe how rude this one seemed with such a direct question. Nyssa turned to Aleria for help with the situation, but her traveling companion had her eyes closed and her whole face scrunched.

She did not want to be as rude as the unicorn, but demanded from Aleria, "What are you doing?"

Aleria stopped concentrating. She opened her eyes and appeared to blush slightly. She looked embarrassed at being caught in this activity. She said, "Trying to turn into one."

"One what? One of us?" asked the blue-eyed unicorn.

"Uh-huh," said Aleria, with a show of innocent confidence.

"It's not working too well," said Nyssa, placing a hand on her friend's shoulder.

Aleria stopped fidgeting entirely, apparently resolved to remain human. She asked, "Sorry, what's happening?"

The lead unicorn filly stamped at the grass. She said, "I asked what are you doing in my meadow?"

Aleria looked genuinely excited and launched a barrage of her own questions, "This is your meadow? I've never seen it before. It's beautiful. What are you? The leader? The queen unicorn?"

"I am Sayonya," answered the unicorn. She raised her head high, the muscles rippled in her long neck. "I need no other title than that. And yes, this is my meadow." The other unicorns made subtle noises and clicked their hooves. Sayonya added, "At least, it will be when I'm old enough."

The other fillies giggled behind Sayonya. She swatted her tail at them and the noise stopped. Apparently, Sayonya was in line to be their leader, but she acted like so many other teenage girls Nyssa met in high school. She told white lies to make herself seem more important. It only made it worse when she actually was someone important.

Nyssa noticed the older members of the herd stopped running. They spread out and rested at the north end of the meadow. Nyssa turned to look at them and Sayonya moved to block her gaze.

"Oh." This startled Nyssa. She did not want to upset the unicorns, but she thought maybe she should not tell the whole truth herself. She answered Sayonya's original question by saying, "We are traveling west and hoped to get a ride."

All of the animals took a step back and Nyssa even saw Aleria's eyes get wide.

Sayonya said, "A ride? A human would dare ask a unicorn for a ride?"

If an animal could look indignant and offended, Sayonya definitely did. Aleria jumped in, "No. No. Forget she said anything. It's not a problem. We would never..."

Sayonya neighed loudly to stop Aleria's rambling. Afraid to look her in the eyes, Nyssa looked to the rest of the herd again. This time, she spotted something that did not belong. Nyssa pointed at three horses entering the clearing from the far side of the meadow. She asked, "What about those three? They don't look like unicorns. Could we ask them for a ride?"

Two large horses, one as gold as wheat and the other as gray as a storm cloud, led the way across the meadow followed by a smaller horse, as black as a moonless night.

"Those fools?" scoffed Sayonya. "Be my guest. They are only concerned for themselves and doubtfully will be of any use."

Regardless of Sayonya's admonishing, Nyssa planned to ask the new horses for help. Since the horses came directly across the meadow to the fillies, that made it easier for her. This close, Nyssa saw that the two older horses towered over her. Nyssa suddenly felt intimidated by the powerful-looking stallions. The younger black horse seemed friendlier as he came up next to Sayonya.

"My name's Wrath. Are you girls lost?" asked the black colt. He seemed sure of himself and a little brash. Nyssa knew plenty of boys like this back in high school too. That kind easily got in trouble and probably would never amount to anything. She did not like to see those kinds of behaviors coming from the animals in this world.

Sayonya started, "They were hoping for a ride to the west. Can you believe they asked me?"

The dark gray horse looked down at Sayonya. He said, "That's enough, child. It is not your nature to be so arrogant. Have Gulfaxi and I taught you nothing?"

The gold horse, apparently called Gulfaxi, swatted his tail silently. It shocked Nyssa to learn these two mighty horses were some kind of teachers to Sayonya. Only a minute before, she spoke about them like they were selfish and lazy.

"But Dapplegrim, they're strangers. I didn't mean anything by it," said Sayonya defensively.

Dapplegrim. Nyssa loved the sound of the gray horse's name. The name sounded as strong as he looked.

"It is especially important to take heed of strangers," continued Dapplegrim. "You young ones never remember the old stories I tell. How many of Empyrean's queens came to us as strangers? You could be standing before greatness and not even know it."

Now, Nyssa took her turn to scoff. She liked the idea of being called great. She never felt great before and never expected to later. She briefly toyed with the idea of Queen Nyssa and then easily dismissed it. She did not believe she had what it would take to be a queen. No one in her life ever encouraged her to be more than plain old Nyssa.

Wrath, the colt, looked smug. He said, "You better listen to him Sayonya. That work horse's been around way too long. He knows about the old days."

Dapplegrim reared up on his hind legs. Nyssa feared he could easily crush any one of them with his size. The younger animals moved clear as he dropped back on all fours. He snapped, "Watch your mouth boy or I'll put a bit in it."

Wrath looked a little concerned and reeled in his attitude. He said, "Sorry big fella. You know everything I know I learned from you."

The older horse shook out his mane. He said, "You may have heard my lessons, but you haven't learned anything yet. Gulfaxi and I will pass into the twilight soon, then the Northern Friesians will have only you to turn to."

"But I'm still a colt," argued Wrath.

"And soon you will be a general like your father," assured Dapplegrim. "Until then, you are mine to train. For now, go prance about the field with the fillies."

The unicorns responded to that instruction. As they galloped away, Nyssa could hear them laughing like children who narrowly missed a severe scolding.

"Human child, what is it you ask of us?" said Dapplegrim, once the others had gone.

Still nervous, mostly because of his size, Nyssa said, "We hoped not to have to walk all the way to the west. We did not mean to offend anyone."

The old horse flicked his ears. He said, "Never mind that. Do you know where you are going? All the way to the land of the Western Sun?"

Nyssa thought back to her flight on the black rock. She recalled the dizzying sights and said, "I believe there is a great prairie beyond the mountains. We are trying to get to a river there."

Gulfaxi, who had yet to speak a word, looked knowingly at Dapplegrim. The gold horse nodded slowly.

"If you are sure, old friend," said Dapplegrim. They must have been life-long friends. Nyssa guessed they were able to communicate with the simplest of gestures and understood each other completely. Dapplegrim continued, "Gulfaxi will take you. He doesn't talk, but he can understand you and he is fast."

"How fast?" asked Aleria. She looked excited at the prospect of riding the giant horse.

The question brought a smile to Dapplegrim's otherwise stoic face. He said, "Child, in his day, even the wind could not catch Gulfaxi."

"There is one other problem," said Nyssa.

Dapplegrim lowered his head even with hers. He said, "When you have lived as long as I have, you come to realize there is nothing so permanent to cause worry or be called a problem. Only questions to answer and tasks to be done. Gulfaxi and I live by a lost code of honor from a time before. We do not volunteer our services lightly and never relent at the first sign of peril. Gulfaxi is now honor bound to carry you and he shall even if our paths do not cross again."

Gulfaxi knelt for the girls to mount his bare back. Nyssa stopped to pat his nose. She said, "That's the problem. Because of me, you probably won't see him again."

Dapplegrim turned to look at the unicorns. The fillies chased Wrath around the meadow. It always seemed to be Sayonya that caught him each time they stopped. Without looking at her, Dapplegrim said to Nyssa, "I have heard stories of a girl who trots through the ages and suspected you might be her. If you do part company with my old friend, at least try to leave him in a happier time."

Aleria already waited on Gulfaxi's back. Nyssa mounted behind her. Neither Dapplegrim nor Gulfaxi told the other goodbye. The silent horse began to gallop west across the meadow. Nyssa could feel old muscles beneath her stir to life as Gulfaxi picked up speed. The incredible pace drew the attention of many of the unicorns and even Wrath. Nyssa thought she glimpsed admiration in the young colt's eyes.

Chapter 15

The First Duel

The exceptionally fast horse powered onward, barely giving Nyssa a chance to take in her surroundings. They passed the Dead Forest in a blur. What little she could see of it, she did not like and felt bad for what became of Aleria's home.

Nyssa turned forward to look at her friend. It took a moment to find Aleria. The girl turned into a tree frog in hopes of having a better grip on Gulfaxi's back. It seemed to be working, except Nyssa had a difficult time spotting the tiny white frog tangled in the horse's thick white mane. She worried that she might not be able to grab Aleria in time if a switch started to happen. She hoped because they were both touching Gulfaxi that all three might switch together.

With her friend safe and secure, Nyssa needed to concentrate on keeping herself on

Gulfaxi's back. The horse's height and width made him better suited for a giant like Odin. Nyssa had no chance of straddling the horse, so she sat with both legs to one side of his sandy-blonde back. She could not squeeze with her legs, so she had only his mane to grip. With the wind whipping in her face, Nyssa feared one wrong bounce would send her flying.

That bounce never came. Gulfaxi never took one wrong step. He cleared small bogs and fallen tree trunks without hesitation. He never stumbled and never slowed.

In the distance, occasionally poking up over the tops of the rotted trees, Nyssa caught sight of some purple and gray ridges. She guessed those to be the mountains that divided the East from the Central Plains, but she could not remember their name. She never expected they would reach them so fast. She had no way of guessing how far Gulfaxi took them.

Then, as if everything in Empyrean plotted against her and wanted her to fail, Gulfaxi stopped when they were so close. Nyssa could see nothing forcing him to stop, but the sudden action flung her forward and for a moment, she could see nothing at all. At the same time, Aleria returned to her human form. The stop and Aleria's change almost threw Nyssa from Gulfaxi's back. The mighty horse did not wince as Nyssa clung to his mane, attempting to keep her balance.

Once Nyssa righted herself, she looked over Aleria's shoulder. The enormous horse stopped short at the edge of a clearing. She could not see anything in the wide-open field that would cause him to delay their journey. However, she hoped he stopped far enough back into the tree line to keep them from being spotted if there was someone. Nyssa did not want anybody else slowing their progress.

If Nyssa could have seen Aleria's face, it looked almost as white as her hair. Aleria mumbled, "It can't be."

Nyssa looked in the direction that Aleria stared. She missed it at first glance, but looking harder, she saw it. A house sat atop three stout trees. It actually looked more like a small hut than a house, but that was her first impression. Somehow, in her head, her idea of it changed instantly. It felt to Nyssa like she was having a memory of something she had not experienced yet. She looked again and clearly saw only the hut. The round building blended well with the dead trees behind it, but she could make out a single door and a thatched roof made from dry sticks.

Looking down from the tree house, Nyssa saw something else she missed before. In the middle of the clearing, a hunched figure draped in rags appeared to be yelling at the house.

"I said come here this instant," demanded the cracked voice of an old woman.

Nyssa watched in amazement as the three trees holding the house began to move. Looking at the trees, she realized something about them. Standing still, they looked like trees, but now moving, they looked more like chicken legs. She watched the claws dig into the ground with each step, burying themselves like tree roots. They pulled up weeds and dirt as the yanked free for the next step.

"It can't be her," Aleria repeated in a whisper.

Nyssa matched her whisper, "Who is it?"

"Baba Yaga," answered Aleria.

This name sent a shiver through Gulfaxi and Nyssa felt it as his whole back shook and his tail flicked. Nyssa knew this name from Aleria's stories and she knew it was not good.

With Aleria's words, the old woman spun toward them, displaying some unexpected agility. She stared into the woods almost like she heard her name spoken. The cold stare stirred Nyssa's insides. She suspected if the woman looked directly at them she might have screamed. As the woman scanned the clearing, Nyssa waited tensely. Neither her, Aleria nor Gulfaxi made a sound. Nyssa did not think she could possibly move while that old woman looked in her direction.

Eventually, Baba Yaga turned her attention back to the moving house. By now, it had walked over and knelt in front of her like a gigantic puppy. A flexible staircase unrolled out of the doorway like a wagging tongue. This completed the puppy dog image in Nyssa's mind. For an instant, warm, grandmotherly thoughts replaced the cold feelings emanating from the old woman. Baba Yaga hobbled up the narrow wooden steps and disappeared into the hut.

"You can go now," came the shrill voice from inside the hut, presumably instructing the house to leave. The grandmotherly feelings disappeared.

The hut stretched its chicken legs one at a time. Then it started walking out of the clearing, back toward where Nyssa first saw it.

"Yaga!" shouted a new voice.

From the opposite end of the clearing, an approaching woman yelled again, "Baba Yaga, you are not getting away that easily."

This woman looked very much the same as Baba Yaga from what Nyssa could see. She seemed friendlier at first glance. Other than that, she had the same stringy hair and wrinkled skin. She carried a walking stick, unlike the first old woman. Nyssa wondered if they could be sisters.

"What?" came Baba Yaga's voice from inside the house. "Who's calling me? Is that you Hulda?"

"You know it is, you old worm," said the woman crossing the field.

"Who is Hulda?" Nyssa asked Aleria in a hushed voice.

Aleria did not answer right away. The look on her face did not reassure Nyssa. Finally, Aleria answered, "She must be Mother Hulda. Another one of your fairytales, like the Prismata." Even with proof, Nyssa wondered if Aleria would ever believe her.

The house turned around so that the open door faced Mother Hulda. Baba Yaga appeared in the doorway. Nyssa could see them both now at the same time and they did look almost identical.

The only difference she could see was Baba Yaga's face looked loose, like a poorly fitting mask.

"What do you want now, Hulda?" Baba Yaga said from her superior perch.

Mother Hulda stood up as straight as her old bones would allow. Nyssa thought she looked quite upset. Hulda said, "You give me back my skin."

"Ha," scoffed Yaga. "You were done with it." She seemed to dismiss Hulda and headed back into her mobile home.

Hulda looked to be mumbling to herself, "Maybe I was, maybe I wasn't. If somebody sheds their skin, that doesn't give somebody else the right to take it. It's my skin and I will do with it as I please."

Then Mother Hulda raised her walking stick like a baseball bat. She reeled back and struck one of the bulky chicken legs. The house stopped in its tracks. It shuddered so violently that some of the sticks fell from the thatched roof. The house dropped to its knees. From inside, Nyssa could hear Baba Yaga give a yelp.

"Nice hit," cheered Aleria. As soon as she said it, Aleria slapped her hands over her mouth like a surprised child. Nyssa could see Mother Hulda's face and knew at least she heard the yell. When Baba Yaga poked her head out of the open door, she knew they both did. This time, Hulda and Yaga looked directly at them.

"No sense hiding any longer," Nyssa said to Gulfaxi. She truly did not want any more delays, but hiding from two women who were most likely witches seemed more dangerous. Maybe by showing themselves, they could move on sooner, she hoped. The big golden horse sauntered into the clearing.

"Delicious," said Yaga, when they were in full view.

"No you don't," ordered Hulda. "They will leave us in the same manner in which they came to us – skin in place and all of their fingers and toes."

Nyssa did not like the way Baba Yaga continued to stare at them. She looked hungry. Mother Hulda's words did not make her feel any better. If Baba Yaga stole people's skin and thought young girls looked delicious, she definitely did not want to stay for lunch.

"Come down to me, dears," said Mother Hulda. She leaned on her stick and beckoned with her free hand.

Nyssa felt like they could trust her more than Yaga and nudged Gulfaxi. He knelt for the girls to dismount. On the ground, they kept their distance from both women. Nyssa looked to Gulfaxi. His expression showed concern, but not worry. She believed the great horse would not let them come to harm.

"Come. Come closer," said Hulda. "I don't bite, unlike some."

Mother Hulda appeared to be friendly, up close. She seemed like an innocent grandmother. The same feeling Nyssa briefly felt from Baba Yaga. Maybe it was some sort of entrapment spell, Nyssa wondered. Looking back at Yaga hanging out of her doorway, she decided it was not. While she momentarily felt that way about Baba Yaga, she did not now. Hulda already accused Yaga of being a thief and she hinted that the woman in the hut wanted to eat the girls. Besides that, Nyssa felt funny when she looked closer at Yaga. The best way she could describe it was *squirmy*, like flipping over a big rock to watch the bugs scatter.

Nyssa led the way toward Hulda. Aleria followed, tucked safely behind her friend and holding her hand. Nyssa knew Aleria had to be terrified being so close to the woman that cursed her. She did not know the whole story, but she did not want it to end here. She could feel Aleria trembling even in her hand.

"What are you looking at?" Yaga snapped down at Aleria.

The younger girl ducked further behind Nyssa. She whimpered, "Nothing, ma'am."

The old woman eyed them both. A small dot formed at the corner of her eye like a black tear. It started to roll slowly down her cheek, stopped, turned and crawled up her nostril. Yaga did not flinch. Nyssa would have screamed if a bug crawled across her cheek. Who knows what she would have done if it went up her nose. It appeared perfectly normal and comfortable for Baba Yaga to have one creep out of her eye and stroll across her face. This bothered Nyssa. It bothered her a lot.

"Go inside," Hulda said to the girls. "We will have tea."

Nyssa thought it was a bad idea, but she could not resist Mother Hulda. Her feet seemed to move at the woman's command instead of by her own will.

"Too bad there won't be any snacks," added Yaga as the stair case unrolled to welcome them.

The girls waited behind Mother Hulda as the old woman hobbled up the steps. Nyssa took the opportunity to whisper to Aleria.

"Did you see the way Baba Yaga looked at you?" Nyssa realized something and she only had this one chance to share it.

"She looked ready to eat," said Aleria.

"Not that," said Nyssa. "She didn't recognize you. We must have switched back to a time before she cursed you."

Aleria looked pleasantly surprised. She said, "That means she doesn't know what I can do."

"She doesn't know what either of us can do," added Nyssa.

"That might come in handy," said Aleria.

As soon as the girls entered the hut, mostly against their will, the stairs rolled up and the legs extended to their full height. The wobbling building stood much higher than Gulfaxi, but did not feel nearly as steady. Inside, the room appeared nothing like the outside. Nyssa could not believe how much larger it was. Also, it looked nothing like a round hut. The house had four bare walls, like a cabin with an enormous stone fireplace opposite the door. Other than a wobbly wooden table in the middle of the room, Nyssa saw no other furniture.

"Sit down," ordered Yaga. She pointed at the side wall. Where Nyssa saw nothing a moment ago, she now found four chairs, as poorly crafted as the table, hanging on steel hooks that seemed to grow out of the wall.

Aleria helped Nyssa put the chairs around the table, careful not to move more than an arm's length away. They made sure the two older women sat first. Then they arranged their own chairs on the opposite side of the table. Nyssa could not explain the compelling feeling she had to do this although she did not want to be there. Maybe it was *bad magic*.

Baba Yaga slowly moved her arm over the table. Her hanging sleeve brushed the table top and as she moved, four cups of tea appeared in the wake of her arm. Nyssa did not want to drink, but she felt like she had to.

Before picking up her own cup, Mother Hulda asked, "What brings you through my woods?"

Yaga added, "Our woods."

Hulda rapped her cane on the table. "My woods. I am not gone yet and you have no real power without me."

Baba Yaga looked offended. She seemed to have more to say, but apparently decided not to speak.

"Are you sisters?" asked Nyssa. She tried to change the subject to keep from revealing her quest.

"Ha! She wishes," said Yaga with a cackle.

Hulda stood. "I am Mother Hulda, seer and teacher. For two hundred years, I have watched these woods like my mother before me. I may not be liked by all, but I am fair. If I force you into something unpleasant, it is for your own good in the end."

Hulda looked proud. Nyssa understood a little better. She believed Mother Hulda put a spell on her and Aleria to force them into the hut with Yaga. She could not guess why the old woman did it, but she did not think they were meant to become food for the other witch. Yaga laughed at Hulda's speech like it was the funniest thing she ever heard. Nyssa could not decide if she liked either of these women.

When Hulda sat, she gently wrapped her skinny fingers around the handle of her tea cup. She sipped carefully at the hot beverage. Steam hid her face, but Nyssa noticed an odd reaction through the vapor.

"This imposter here," Hulda pointed at Yaga, "is nothing but a creeping collection of lies."

That statement brought Yaga's howls of laughter under control. She snickered a little still, but focused on Hulda.

"Oh? Lies, eh? Want to know a piece of truth?" said Yaga.

She apparently noticed that neither Nyssa nor Aleria touched their tea. Suddenly, Nyssa felt a strange sense of relief for not drinking.

Yaga said, "The truth is, I wish you all would have had a sip."

Hulda made the same contorted face Nyssa saw a moment ago, obscured by the steam. She sat her cup down and stumbled back from her chair. Mother Hulda swung her cane wildly, smashing all of the teacups. Yaga leapt backwards from her chair with the same surprising agility Nyssa witnessed earlier.

"Poison!" shouted Mother Hulda. "How dare you!" Hulda charged at Baba Yaga.

"It was your own fault for trusting me," said Yaga.

Before the tip of her outstretched hand reached Yaga, Hulda's entire body seized. Her skin instantly dried and she collapsed into a pile of dirt on the floor. Baba Yaga turned toward the girls revealing her pointed teeth and clawed hands. She squealed, "Now we eat."

"Run," Aleria demanded to Nyssa. A second later, she transformed into a huge, white grizzly bear.

Yaga jumped back in surprise, giving both girls a chance to make it out the door. They stood on a narrow ledge, almost twenty feet off the ground. Nyssa saw Gulfaxi galloping toward them. He must have sensed the danger. Aleria kept watch on the door, but Yaga did not follow. Hulda's spell no longer controlled Nyssa's movements and she pulled her friend from the ledge. In mid-air, Aleria turned human again and they landed roughly on Gulfaxi's back. He broke into a gallop immediately without question.

Baba Yaga screamed at her hut, "What are you waiting for? Get them!"

Nyssa looked over her shoulder to see the hut take a few steps. Gulfaxi had not made it to full speed yet. The chicken legs crouched under the hut and sprang into the air. She watched the hut easily sail over their heads, one leg leading and the other two trailing behind.

The hut landed on all three legs, blocking their path. The chicken claws smashed into the ground. Nyssa felt small bits of dirt hit her face as shrapnel from the impact. Then the house reared up on its two back legs. It bent the front leg for a deadly strike.

The dirt must have gotten in Nyssa's eyes, because her vision became blurry and she could not see anything. The sudden raging headache told her it was not dirt in her eyes, but rather a coming switch.

"Hold on," Nyssa yelled to Aleria. She squeezed Gulfaxi's neck and felt her friend's arms around her waist.

Nyssa could barely make out the giant claws streaking for them. Then she saw only green trees. She fell from Gulfaxi's back to the soft grass that replaced the weedy clearing. Nyssa did not know if she was going to throw up or pass out next.

She did both.

Chapter 16

The First Prisoner

When Nyssa woke, she saw only blue sky. Then her friend's face filled her vision.

"Are you okay?" asked Aleria. Nyssa could feel Aleria holding her right hand. "Don't try to move."

"I'm fine," Nyssa said as she rose to a sitting position. She actually did feel fine. She guessed she must have been asleep for a while, the switching pain in her head had gone completely.

Nyssa looked around and made two realizations. First, she knew they had switched safely away from Baba Yaga. The rich green forest looked young and alive. There was no sign of the creepy walking hut or any sound of that cackling hag. Thinking of Yaga's sagging skin gave her a chill. She wondered what it was about the woman's skin that did not seem right, almost as if something crawled beneath the surface.

In her other realization, she now understood that Aleria truly was her friend. She could not remember when she started thinking of the shape-shifting girl as her friend. Somewhere along their journey, it happened on its own. For too long, Nyssa grew used to having no friends. She never had anyone to force her out of her protective shell, never encourage her to do something different. In her old life, she never had anyone with which to share her music or a simple laugh.

Of all places, this strange land of Empyrean gave her that. She finally had a real friend and that terrified her. With one switch, she could lose that friend forever.

Aleria must have sat with her the entire time she was unconscious. She had no idea how long, but the sun was still shining. Nyssa hoped her episode did not waste too much time. She felt that the switches might be starting to get dangerous for her. She imagined several things that could happen if she fainted at the wrong time. It scared her, but she also realized that switching had now saved her more than once. She also managed to stay with her friend. Because of that, the risks did not seem as bad.

With the surrounding forest in full bloom, Nyssa assumed they had gone back in time, perhaps back before Baba Yaga existed. She could not guess how far back, though. No rainbow graced the azure sky. That told her the Prismata were not up there. Nyssa had a suspicion that they went so far back that the Prismata had not yet ascended. She felt like maybe they were close to the beginning, close to the start of Empyrean. If Empyrean had a time of creation, this could have been it. Or, at least, close, but she had no proof.

A thump on the ground behind her caught Nyssa attention. Gulfaxi stamped the ground. He waited patiently. Nyssa realized that the loyal horse switched with them. This made her thankful. She discovered there was an awful lot of walking to be done in Empyrean. If Gulfaxi was willing to carry them, she was willing to ride.

"We should keep moving," said Nyssa. She tried to stand, but Aleria would not let her.

"You sit, for a moment. Whatever is happening to you, I think it's getting worse," said Aleria.

"I'm fine," argued Nyssa, even though she had the same thoughts only a moment before.

Aleria pushed her back to her seat on the ground. "No, you're not. Do *fine* people turn invisible?"

"What?" This startled Nyssa. She shot her free hand up in front of her face. She could see it clearly. "What are you talking about? I'm not invisible."

Aleria looked worried. "You started to disappear. You were asleep for almost an hour and started to vanish. It must have been a switch. I grabbed your hand and haven't let go since."

Nyssa squeezed Aleria's hand in hers. Despite the smallest remnants of a headache, she honestly felt fine. She said, "I feel alright now."

"I don't want you to leave me," said Aleria.

Nyssa thought she saw tears in the younger girl's eyes. In that moment, Nyssa felt their bond strengthen into something more than friends. She knew Aleria felt the same about her and that they would stay together. In that moment, they became sisters.

"I won't ever let you go," Nyssa said, swallowing hard. She believed any tears now would cause her headache to swell.

When Aleria finally agreed to let Nyssa move, the girls walked, holding hands. Nyssa did not want to take too much advantage of Gulfaxi, so they followed behind him as he forged a path through the beautiful woods. Nyssa listened to the sounds of the young forest. She heard birds somewhere in the distance. Something like a bee even buzzed past her ear. They walked on into the evening until they came to a wide roadway that ran alongside a huge mountain range. The mountains stretched away in either direction as far as Nyssa could see. The well-maintained road made Nyssa wonder if they had travelled back as far as she thought.

"This has to be the Mountain ByWay," said Aleria. "There's only one safe pass through the Euphoric Mountains, in my time, anyway."

Nyssa shuddered at the memory of her encounter with Raymond Shaydaway. She said, "I still don't like the idea of travelling on the road. There has to be another way over the mountains. Maybe even a tunnel?"

Aleria looked aggravated. She said, "No. There are no tunnels. You never go into the tunnels."

That seemed like a sore subject. Nyssa suspected that Aleria must have had a bad experience in a tunnel or heard some awful stories.

"We can follow the Byway to the Great Road. It is the safest and fastest way," continued Aleria. "Do you want to climb that?"

She pointed up the drastically sloping mountainside. For the first time since being in sight of them, Nyssa studied the sheer rock walls. The mountains appeared to have passable slopes in only a few places. Steep, jagged edges covered most of this face along the length of the road. With the setting sun glaring on the rock, she could see ledges and crevasses. It would be dark soon and that would make the climb a real challenge. Nyssa did not think it would be impossible for her or Aleria, but it seemed very difficult. Then she thought about Gulfaxi. She knew it would take a truly amazing horse to climb the easiest parts of these mountains. She could not imagine a horse ever climbing so high. That helped her decide that Aleria was right. The only way they would make it safely to the other side of the mountains would be to use the roads, exposed or not.

"We will take the Great Road then," agreed Nyssa.

Gulfaxi knelt for the girls to mount. Before he made it to a full gallop, a noise caught their attention. A sudden crumbling of rocks caused Gulfaxi to stop. The girls watched as he looked toward the mountains on their left. His ears flicked forward as if he expected danger. Nyssa strained to see only a handful of pebbles rolling down in a few spots. She saw no other movement and expected it to simply be natural erosion from wind up high on the mountain.

Then, something else caught her eye. She thought it looked like a hairless cat standing on its hind legs. Nyssa immediately decided it was not a cat. While it had a cat's ears and tail, its skin looked much darker and its front, or upper, paws looked more human with sharp claws.

The creature scrunched its face and let out a giggle that instantly annoyed Nyssa, "He, he, ha, ha, he."

In the brief moment that it giggled, more of the odd things joined the first. Nyssa saw that no two of them looked exactly alike, but they all seemed to be related. Ten of these creatures ranged in size from the first cat-like one, to a pair as big as herself. They all had green, hairless skin that appeared to glisten with mucous or some slime. Some wore rudimentary armor and helmets, while a few wore nothing at all. They laughed and snickered their annoying, taunting laughs as they stared at Nyssa and her friends. They seemed to know a secret that Nyssa did not want to know.

"Everywhere we go, you bring more of these things," Aleria said to Nyssa.

"What do you mean?" asked Nyssa.

"You and your *make believe* creatures. I think these are goblins, like my mom used to tell me about. I always thought it was to keep me from playing on the sharp rocks. They're not supposed to be real."

More laughter echoed from above, hidden behind jagged outcroppings. Nyssa could not tell how many waited in hiding, but it far outnumbered the ten they could see.

"We should go," suggested Nyssa.

Before Gulfaxi could respond, two of the biggest goblins leapt the short distance from the rocks to the horse. The goblins knocked the girls from Gulfaxi's back. In that instant, the other goblins pounced. They struck at both girls with rocks and sticks. The world became a storm of slimy arms and legs. Two or three started pulling Nyssa by the hair. They dragged her toward the mountainside as Aleria tumbled in the other direction. Nyssa did not want to be too far from her friend.

As the goblins hoisted Nyssa onto the rocks, she saw them now dragging Aleria in the same direction. Despite the situation, Nyssa felt some relief that Aleria was close. However, the goblins did not seem to be interested in Gulfaxi. That did not stop him from trampling the one that looked like a cat. Then more goblins started to appear. They worked together to lift Nyssa and Aleria higher up onto the rocks. Reinforcements appeared to keep Gulfaxi away with sharp weapons like small swords and short spears.

Faster than she could realize, the goblins had Nyssa at least fifty feet up the sheer wall. They climbed with ease, even carrying the girls. They found hand holds and foot holds that seemed impossible. Down below, Gulfaxi hoofed at the rocks, only to slide back down to the road. Nyssa knew he could not climb. She knew he could not get to them now. She hoped maybe he knew some other way to save them.

She yelled, "Try to find help."

Gulfaxi looked in several directions. Apparently, he decided north would be best and galloped out of sight.

The goblins carried the girls higher. They seemed to have no problem dealing with the struggling girls while keeping their grips on the dangerous mountainside. More and more goblins appeared as they went higher. Nyssa thought she should have been terrified. Instead, she gave up struggling and let a certain calmness wash over her. This made her think for a moment why they called this place the Euphoric Mountains.

About the time Nyssa could no longer see the road below, they leveled off and the goblins headed down a pass deeper into the hidden recesses of the mountains. Even if Gulfaxi could find help, Nyssa expected that help could never find them.

The goblins, cackling the entire time, moved in a single file line through the narrow pass. Nyssa could catch an occasional glimpse of Aleria on the backs of the goblin's ahead of her. She could not, however, see why Aleria started shouting, "No, no, no!" After a moment, she understood when the goblins carried them both into a small tunnel.

For an instant, all was black. Then fear replaced Nyssa's unnatural calm. Before they went too far, the goblins stopped their laughing and lit torches. The green flames reflecting off the purple stone of the walls made Nyssa feel worse, almost sick to her stomach. Now in silence, the assorted goblins heavy and irregular breathing did not help her feeling. The only comforting thing Nyssa found was that the tunnel widened as they went deeper.

Finally, they made it to a large chamber that appeared to be the goblins' home. Around the edges of the deep side of the room, Nyssa saw piles of animal skins that must have been their beds. Baby goblins cooed on one of the piles near their mother. They would have been cute, except Nyssa already knew what they would grow up to be. She thought the babies looked quite human, except for their green skin. She guessed humans and goblins might be related somehow. She wondered what horrible thing might have happened to twist them into such creatures.

The goblins unceremoniously threw their prisoners into a cage that looked almost as if it grew out of the stone wall. Stalactites and stalagmites must have fused together to create the wide-spaced bars. Unfortunately, neither Nyssa nor Aleria could squeeze through them as they immediately attempted. The mysterious purple stone somehow even formed the cage door which the goblins slammed shut and locked with a hidden key.

Now ignoring their prisoners, the goblins began to feast on the uncooked meat of some small forest creatures that Nyssa did not recognize. At least, she thought, the goblins had enough sense to keep their eating area away from their sleeping area. That was her last thought before the headache that preceded the switch started. She barely had time to grab Aleria.

After the blur faded, but right before she passed out, Nyssa saw no sign of the goblins, but they were still trapped in the same stone prison.

Nyssa awoke to a familiar clicking and whirring sound. With the switching pain reduced to a dull ache, she sat up quickly to find Aleria at her side.

"Easy," said Aleria with a worried tone.

For the moment, Nyssa ignored her friend and scanned their cage for the familiar sound. Outside the cage, in the larger chamber, she spotted the comforting blue light. The eyes of the nightingale illuminated a small area occupied by an unusual looking man.

"It's good to see you again," Nyssa mumbled to the mechanical bird.

The nightingale chirped.

"Oh, he says he's never met you before," volunteered the man with the slightest hint of what Nyssa would call a German accent.

She thought about this for a moment. Nyssa realized that because of her random switching, she must have met the bird in her past, but his future. Maybe it tried to tell her that last time they were together, but she could not understand the chirps.

Tym must have realized this was very confusing to his audience. He took a moment to explain it to Zandria, Olena and their friends. The nightingale had a normal timeline, in which it first met Nyssa in the cave prison. When they were together in the forest, that was the bird's future. Ironically, Nyssa's first meeting was the bird's second and the other way around for the bird. The two meetings were hundreds of years apart, but the nightingale's steam-powered mechanical parts allowed him to continue clicking and chirping for ages.

Nyssa saw the nightingale's blue eyes focused on the man like a theatre spotlight. She studied his long, pointed beard and long, stringy hair. He looked well-dressed, but dirty, like he had not changed clothes in some time. The actual style of his clothes reminded Nyssa of something out of a Cinderella fairytale. He looked like he belonged in a royal court with his frilled cuffs and long coat tails. He sat cross-legged with his pot belly resting on his knees, apparently waiting for Nyssa to awaken.

"It seems you may have met my creation some time before," said the man. "It is not likely that you would confuse him with another as he is the only one of his kind."

"Maybe," said Nyssa, trying to make sense of it. She wiped the last of the sleep from her eyes. She would definitely know *her* nightingale anywhere, but the man referred to it as *his* creation. Nyssa tried to guess how far they switched this time. She knew they switched forward enough for the goblins to be long gone, but not as far as her first meeting with the nightingale. That gave her a couple hundred years in between maybe.

She asked, "How did you find us here?"

Aleria answered first, "He fell through a hole in the ceiling."

Nyssa looked up, finally noticing the small cone of sunlight that added to the nightingale's spotlight.

"Well, that is slightly more simple than I would describe it," said the man. "First, I should introduce myself. I am Doktor Allwissend, Inventor and Healer. I hail from the court of the Queen of the Western Sun and am on a fact-finding quest of the other realms of Empyrean. My eventual goal is to travel beyond our borders and bring back knowledge of the other lands of Zakaria."

"What is Zakaria?" asked Nyssa.

"My dear child," began Doktor Allwissend with some surprise. He used the gentle, correcting voice of a teacher, "Zakaria is the world on which we live, weaved together by our dreams and beliefs. Surely you did not think Empyrean existed only by itself. There are many other lands to the north, south, west and even east beyond the great sea."

"I'm still getting used to the idea that Empyrean is real," said Nyssa. She thought it made sense that there could be a world beyond Empyrean. She did not want to think of it as her only concern for now dealt with this one cave.

Doktor Allwissend continued, "As I was saying, I intend to explore all of Empyrean first. As such, I found the Euphoric Mountains to be delightful. It seems their power is only effective above ground. Something to do with erosion, I expect. Down here, or in here, I feel no effects of euphoria whatsoever."

"That's great information to have," said Aleria. "But do you think you could investigate a way to get us out of here?"

The peculiar explorer said, "You do seem to be in a predicament. I was walking through the mountain pass and only accidently stepped on a soft spot that delivered me here. It seems that my greatest discoveries always happen by chance. In any event, it appears I need a very specific key to open your cage."

Nyssa remember the words of the messenger squirrel Rata. He told her the nightingale would set her free once she set it free. It started to make sense now. She stuck out a finger, beckoning the mechanical bird. It flew to her with its gently clicking wings.

"He's never done that before," mused Doktor Allwissend.

As quickly as the nightingale landed on her finger, Nyssa told Aleria, "Time to go. She felt the switch coming, but did not warn the explorer. Aleria instantly understood, though, and grabbed ahold of Nyssa's arm a moment before it happened.

After the switch, Nyssa fought the overpowering urge to faint. Her stomach hurt, but she managed to give some instructions to the nightingale before dry heaving.

"Go, my friend. Be free and bring us help," said Nyssa.

The nightingale flew about the room that was once again full of goblins. The room looked almost identical to when they previously left and they must have switched back to about the same time, Nyssa guessed. The goblins looked confused and growled angrily. Nyssa fought the stomach pain and growing headache long enough to see the nightingale escape and then she was unconscious.

After an indeterminable haze, Nyssa awoke to a room full of new creatures. They carried their own orange-flamed torches and glowing amulets of bright yellow. Nyssa welcomed this sight over the green goblin flames although the brightness made her squint. All about the room, goblins lay motionless, pierced with arrows. Nyssa could not even hear a sound from the goblin babies, but, thankfully, she did not see them anywhere either. Nyssa found the nightingale perched on the shoulder of the creature that appeared to be the leader of their rescuers.

He looked mostly human, except far taller. His ears looked as pointed as his fingernails and his black eyes beamed with intensity. His thick black hair hung over his shoulder in a braid that reminded her of the Native Americans she studied in school.

"The elves saved us," declared Aleria.

The leader of these elves used his sword to break the lock on their prison. He said, "If not for your little friend here, we never would have found you. These goblin nests are well hidden in the mountains."

Chapter 17

The First Hawks

"This is too unbelievable," said Adam. He jumped up from his seat in apparent anticipation.

Zandria then watched her friend Dew move right in front of Tym. She looked ready to attack him.

Dew said, "Finally. Elves finally get into the story and that's where you decide to take a break? Who said you could take a break anyway? You at least have to tell which clan rescued her."

Tym appeared flustered by the sudden commotion. He must have gotten used to hearing his own voice for so long with such a silent audience. Zandria truly was enthralled and thought Tym was a wonderful storyteller, almost as good as Kez.

"It doesn't say," Tym answered. He double-checked the book again.

"What?" replied Dew. "A clan of elves saved the first queen and it doesn't say which one? Surely one of the clans laid claim to this honor?"

"To my knowledge, no. The clans were different then," said Tym. The tone of his voice was absolute. He added, "Sometime before the Passing Queen, our kind distanced themselves from the humans. No one ever claimed the rescue. If it eases your mind, the Lantispheres are mentioned by name a few chapters from now."

This seemed to appease Dew. She returned to her seat with an accomplished grin. Adam still paced behind his chair. Zandria could barely hear him mumbling to himself.

"This can't be the same William. That would make him at least five hundred years old. He's never said anything about any of this as far as I can remember," Adam finished.

Zandria remembered though. She remembered finding William in that garden, frozen solid. She remembered Olena freeing him with her magic mirror. Together they crossed the same Wastelands to the same unicorn meadow. The thought of Nyssa's encounter with Baba Yaga gave her chills. Zandria began to feel a strange connection to Nyssa. It seemed that Nyssa and Aleria shared a similar journey, and relationship, with Zandria and her sister. Zandria wished she could somehow meet Nyssa, but that would be impossible. Zandria knew the story affected Olena. She still hung on Zandria's arm which started to make it fall asleep.

"May I have my arm back, Your Majesty?" joked Zandria to her sister.

"Oh." Olena t'sked her tongue against her teeth. "Sorry," followed by an exaggerated grin, as if she was not aware of her hold. She let go and tried to make herself comfortable in a new position.

Eisenhahn, who sat silently for most of the story, raised his hand. No one noticed at first and he continued to wait patiently, without a word.

Zandria spotted his odd behavior first. "Do you have a question or something?"

"Yes," said Eisenhahn with no further elaboration.

Zandria and the others waited for him to ask. After a few more moments of silence, Zandria said, "You can ask it now."

"Thank you," said Eisenhahn. He waited until he carefully lowered his massive arm back to his lap. Then he asked, "When is my part of the story?"

Tym looked to be as sympathetic as possible when he told Eisenhahn, "I'm sorry friend, but you're not in this story."

"But I used to be in stories," explained Eisenhahn. Do you remember the stories the old man told about me? Do you remember him? Wizard L..." Eisenhahn looked puzzled, as if he forgot an old friend's name. The big iron man tried again. "Wizard Lem? Wizard Lark?" He sighed a sigh that nearly broke Zandria's heart. He finished, "I guess it doesn't matter if I'm not in this one. I know I'm in the story about the old lady."

That sounded strange to Zandria. It seemed maybe Eisenhahn learned something from his mysterious old master, but he could not put it into words. Zandria felt bad that too many times, it was easier to dismiss his mixed up words as childish imagination.

Olena also looked a little sad for Eisenhahn. She said, "I have a question then. Who *is* in this story? I mean, so far we've only heard about Nyssa. I thought there were four queens from the very beginning. Can you please tell us about all of them?"

"Excellent question," added Kez.

Tym looked a little surprised. He said, "I can share what I know, but their journals are not kept at Castle Empyrean. Theirs are kept in their homelands."

"Why do you have this one then?" asked Zandria.

"I've never really thought about that," said Tym. "It is substantially larger than the others. Perhaps this one is protected, considering the girl's origins. The other three queens were born in their lands. And technically, the eastern queen was the first of all four of them to become a queen."

Sylvan squeaked, "Most fascinating. Perhaps there is something about the eastern throne that brings us such unique queens from that land?"

Tym agreed, "I do say at least two of them had to go through quite harrowing journeys to become queen."

Kez climbed up on the nearest armrest. He said, "I would love to hear what you know about the other queens. Please, continue."

"I should start at the point where Nyssa arrived and then departed from the giants' battlefield," said Tym. "To my knowledge, the Forgotten Evil broke free from his prison at that point. The four shards of the shattered, enchanted black rock flew to the four realms of Empyrean. As the story is told, the eastern queen became caught up in the force of the blast and was carried to the seashore."

"At the same time, Gilgamesh left to begin his untold quest for the Atumval. He has never been heard of since. This left only three Immortals to fight the Forgotten Evil and his four lieutenants."

"By fortune or fate, the ground beneath the broken prison began to collapse. Within a matter of moments, the Forgotten Evil fell into the bottomless canyon over which we now hang."

"Unfortunately, before he fell, the Forgotten Evil instructed his lieutenants on a new course of action. The dark beasts hastily made their way toward Arcenland in the far south. They would eventually return with an army of countless, angry Carcharodans."

"Odin implored Horus and the Parasauratitan to give chase in hopes of stopping the lieutenants. Neither of those Immortals ever returned from the south. Odin, however, had a different path to walk."

"The white-bearded giant knew of a people that roamed the northern plains and made their homes in the great forests beyond the flat land. He knew they were a spiritual people, living in harmony with the land and its animals. He knew they also had special abilities that would be most helpful."

Dew interrupted with a cheer, "Elves!"

"Yes, elves," concurred Tym. "Odin presented himself to the tribal princess. Before our kind divided into clans, we lived as one tribe under one ruler. When the great ruler passed into the Twilight, the clans already began to separate, but still followed the leadership of his twin daughters, Malika and Marika Lantisphere. The sisters heard Odin's plea and agreed to help."

Zandria thought Dew was about to burst from her seat. She could feel her friend next to her shaking with proud excitement.

Tym continued, "What came forth from those northern plains was the last great gathering of the elven tribe. After the First War for Empyrean, the elves completely divided into smaller clans. Some befriended the queens and humans for a while. Many left Empyrean entirely and a very few clans thrived on the hatred that grew from their losses in the war. These clans turned on their own kind, but were driven from Empyrean."

"Malika and Marika shared visions in their dreams. Until Odin came to them, they had one dream they could not understand. In this dream, four girls stood at the mouth of a cataclysmic pit. The twins knew only these girls could halt some impossible evil from rising out of that pit. With Odin's words, my mother and her sister then understood they had to find these girls at any cost."

"Before many animals learned to talk, our people could already communicate with them. And at that time, there were none more majestic than the giant predatory hawks of the plains.. The elves never knew a faster, more honorable bird than these hawks. They also knew that no elf could search farther or faster than the birds. A request was made and four hawks flew in four directions to find these girls."

Tym stopped.

Then he added, "Of course, the hawks are much smaller now. However, the Empyrical Guard that roosts in our highest towers are descended from those Queen Finders."

"The old giant hawks were called Queen Finders?" asked Ovara.

"They were," said Tym. "And that is what they did. Before I continue the story of the Queen of the Eastern Sky, I will tell you briefly what I know of the North, South and West."

Chapter 18

The First Queen of the Northern Wood

As sure as trees sprouted from the ground, humans populated the wild woods of the north in the earliest days of Empyrean. They came from the far west and built simple small villages throughout the great forests.

These humans did not easily make friends with the animals or elves. The humans were quick to anger and hunted for pleasure, rather than necessity. They tried to live in the many different forests of the Northern Wood, but soon found themselves most suited for the central valley.

Lochnoble grew to become the greatest of their towns, situated on the crest of the valley.

Spreading out from there, smaller villages staked their claims across these woods.

It is in one of these villages, far to the north and west of Lochnoble, that Brynn Gunn was born. The name of her village is long forgotten, as has the wood of their homes long returned to the dirt from which it grew.

Born the only child of a proud huntsman, Brynn learned all the skills of the axe and bow. She became an accomplished hunter by the age of ten. She kept a secret from her father, however. Some unusual creatures called Skiordan, that kept their distance from humans, aided young Brynn in her many hunts.

The Skiordan lived in the treetops of the neighboring forest. While they helped Brynn on the ground, they lived in the trees for good reason. Many of the other strange, ferocious creatures that inhabited this part of the woods could not climb at all.

While Brynn's family and fellow humans struggled to tame the incredible horses of the north, Brynn explored the wild. Her gentle spirit and curiosity allowed her to befriend another northern group disdained by her own kind.

When not hunting, she liked to explore and discovered something struggling in the dirt of her father's attempt at a garden. The wiggling pile of dirt whined, almost like the squeal of a pig, as if the sunlight hurt it. Brynn crouched and cast her shadow over the pile. She brushed away the clumps of dirt to find an unusually small man. She thought, at first, maybe he fell out of a tree like the Skiordan. Then, with no trees close, her mind told her maybe he fell from underground. Being a foot shorter than her, she picked him up with his feet barely off the ground.

"Put me down," the bearded man gruffly demanded.

"What are you?" asked Brynn.

"I could ask the same of you."

Brynn let the man slide from her hands to solid ground. She said, "I'm sorry. My name's Brynn Gunn."

"Gun...gun? Ha," snorted the man. "I am called Lowgun, but we surely are no kin."

That day started a friendship of legend. At first, his visits were infrequent because his people, the dwarves, lived far below ground. Only in recent times did the dwarves surface to lend their skills to Empyrean. Still, they preferred the rock, and some, the dark.

In the short time that Brynn and Lowgun did spend together, he taught her more about the axe than her father did in the first ten years of her life. For her eleventh birthday, Lowgun made her a gift of a very special axe. It had two broad blades facing away from each other. He wrapped the handle in a soft, yet durable, material buttoned on by gold rivets. A small green crystal nestled at the base of the hilt.

Lowgun explained, "That crystal is meant to match your eyes."

Brynn's friends and neighbors praised her skill in crafting her new axe. Sadly, she did not think she could tell them who really made it. In those early days, humans treated the rare above-ground dwarf like an unwanted pest.

Because her father was the village elder, all of their neighbors gathered for Brynn's birthday celebration. They feasted, played games and enjoyed lively music. During the party, several people requested for Brynn to give a demonstration with her new axe.

Her confidence swooned as Brynn listened to the cheers and gasps of awe. With little effort, she sliced through tree trunks thicker even than her father's mighty chest. Then she cut thrown rocks spinning through the air as if they were potatoes. She even excelled at throwing the axe. They put up target after target, each one further than the last. Brynn did not miss a single bullseye, until the last throw.

A tremendous crashing noise broke her concentration. Something tore through the trees not far from their village. It sounded much too large to be made by any of the creatures she knew from the nearby Peckwood Forest, as it had come to be called. Even with the distraction, Brynn still managed to hit the last target, but no bullseye this time.

Leaving the party in dismay and disarray, a group of hunters, naturally including Brynn and her father, headed out into the woods. It did not take them long to find the huge, jagged, black rock with its mysterious silver speckles. As they examined it, none of the men, alone or all together, could even move the rock. They had no guess from where it even came.

Brynn's father decided it must have fallen from the sky by the way the tree tops were shredded and the rock dug down into the ground. In the following days, the villagers agreed to stay away from the rock. They felt it was a bad omen.

Three days after the birthday party, Lowgun found Brynn alone.

"We have examined the rock from underneath," he said. "There is nothing like it in our world. The sages believe it is a sign of change. Something has happened in the land of Empyrean. They believe you are connected to it and hope that you will accept what fate may come."

"What are you talking about? What does that rock have to do with me?" asked Brynn.

Lowgun looked embarrassed. He said, "I don't honestly know. The sages have spent hundreds of years isolated in the deepest caves. They predicted the creation of Empyrean and the coming of you humans. All they will say is that if you are summoned, it would be disastrous to refuse."

"I'm not afraid of a rock," said Brynn. She stood from her tree stump of a seat. She held her axe out in front of her, examining her reflection in the polished metal.

"I do not think it is the rock you have to worry about," finished Lowgun.

Only two days later, a messenger arrived at their village in the form of a giant hawk. The exceptionally large bird startled the men and they drew weapons against it. Brynn stopped them from attacking. She put her small body between the heavily armed men and the fearsome creature. After that moment, it was often said of Brynn that although she was small, she was tough.

The giant hawk spoke in the language taught to him by the elves. The northmen found the language difficult to understand, but it confused them even more that an animal could speak at all. The bird roosted on the thatched roof of a nearby house as the humans struggled to make sense of his words.

What they eventually understood him to say made some sense. "I come from the plains to find that certain maiden. She is much needed."

Her father protested that the bird made no sense, but Brynn knew he lied to protect her. She knew the meaning of the message. She recalled Lowgun's words from only a few days before and believed this was her mission.

She stood up before her village elders and said, "I will go. I believe I am needed for a purpose that will affect us all."

"But you should not go. At least, not alone," said Brynn's father. "This mighty creature may only have set his eyes on you for a meal."

Feeling the well spring of an untapped courage, Brynn said, "Then which of you men will protect this small child?"

The strong hunters of her village turned their eyes to the well-worn dirt of their gathering place. Not one of her kinsmen volunteered.

"I will go," said a voice familiar to Brynn. She looked past the knees of the villagers to find Lowgun the dwarf standing next to her father. "I pledge my life to her safe keeping."

Several of the men looked repulsed by the dwarf. Most, including her father, looked ashamed to lack the bravery shown by the underground dweller, observed Brynn.

With quick preparation and emotional goodbyes, Brynn Gunn mounted the back of the enormous bird. Lowgun found a comfortable spot in her lap and the hawk took wing. They flew south toward the Central Plains.

Chapter 19

The First Queen of the Western Sun

Where the Scarbeck River flows to meet the sunrise is a land of cliffs and canyons. So many canyons, in fact, that some have built their homes on the sheer, steep walls.

They say the canyons are so deep that no one ventures to their depths. They say giants, and worse, live down there.

But the western lands of Empyrean are not all treacherous climbs. Beyond the canyons are countless, beautiful rolling hills. That is where the first people of the Western Sun settled in Empyrean.

Small forests and pristine lakes divided the hills into territories. The aristocratic westerners laid claim to the territories and built their castles on hilltops. These wealthy families forced the commoners to live among the canyons.

These wealthy families also seemed to be always having disputes with each other. A great battle occurred in the first days of the land of the Western Sun. A man, with a magic sword pulled from a stone, built a castle of solid gold and gathered his knights at a round table. Their unhappy neighbors followed them into Empyrean, but the battle ended suddenly. As expected, the man with the magic sword won.

This story is not about that man, but his laws and orders greatly influence the ways of the west even now. This story is also not about that man's wife, although she was known for surpassing beauty. This story is about that beauty's cousin, Elyzabel.

Born in the golden castle, Elyzabel grew up with a life of privilege. She had the best teachers and the best dress-makers. She enjoyed food and music and some leisurely sport.

By the time Elyzabel reached eighteen years of age, she had the opportunity to dismiss many marriage requests. This did not disappoint her parents because she had none. She lived under the care of her beautiful cousin and that cousin's wise husband.

Because of her status in the golden court, the elite asked Elyzabel to judge many challenges and contests. The outcome of these contests often became a source of amusement for her. The kindness of Elyzabel's heart went as deep as the

Canyon of the Silent Echo. She could never find fault in anyone and never wanted to disappoint anyone. Every event she presided over ended in a draw. Even in a joust, when one knight lay on the ground, she praised him for his ability to land safely.

That is why Elyzabel often found herself a guest at that round table. The knights often consulted her before venturing on a quest beyond the borders of Empyrean. The man with the magic sword considered her judgement to be always fair.

Elyzabel only knew the pure gold walls of the castle her entire life. She loved coming to the round table to hear stories of adventure and excitement. The knights seemed to her to be legendary, yet they never spoke of exploring their new home. All of the tales pertained to the old world and not the vast, unexplored Empyrean.

Elyzabel longed to follow the sun and discover the rest of Empyrean.

One evening, when everyone gathered in the great hall for a feast, Elyzabel requested to go to bed early. She did not feel sleepy, but secretly wanted to peer through the ancient magician's forbidden telescope.

Elyzabel knew the old man, if he truly was a man, watched the night sky for signs and portents. He advised her cousin's husband on many a crusade. However, he seemed to disappear frequently and his lab would be empty. Tonight was one of those nights.

The detour Elyzabel chose from her bedroom to the magician's lab took her through the armory. She passed through the armory many times, but seldom had the interest or use of its contents. She honestly had no stomach for swords, shields or spears. However, this night, one sword caught her attention. On the same rack cluttered with ordinary steel swords, she spied the magic sword. She could not believe such an honored weapon that had once been pulled from a sacred stone now lay about so carelessly.

She did not know where, but Elyzabel felt the urge to move the sword somewhere safe, somewhere more respectable. The moment she touched the hilt, light filled her eyes. The wall torches did not sprout more flame, but they suddenly seemed brighter. She could see into the shadowy corners and down the far length of the hall with ease. Everything seemed clearer, both in her eyes and in her mind. Touching the sword, Elyzabel could see the weak points in other swords and shields. The gleaming spots on the walls and square pillars even told her where to strike to cause a collapse. She now had a clarity that gave her an advantage. She suspected this sword could even show her the breaking point of an opponent. She understood how her cousin's husband never lost a battle.

The magic sword spoke to her in her mind, whispering secrets of battle and victory. Wielding this blade, she felt both confident and powerful. She never thought she lacked confidence and never desired to be powerful, but this sword made her feel like she needed both. Now more so, she wondered why this weapon would not be cared for better.

"The power is not in the sword, but in the hand that holds it," said a voice distinctly different from the whisper of the sword.

Elyzabel lashed out with the sword in surprise and self-defense. She demanded, "Who's there?"

"Because my body is elsewhere, does not mean my mind is gone too," said the wizard. Elyzabel, rapidly recovering from her initial fright, now recognized the old man's voice. She thought the sword helped her regain focus faster than she would have on her own.

"I'm sorry," she started. "I didn't mean to..."

"There is nothing for which to apologize," said the wizard. "The sword speaks to those that need to hear its voice. It is not for one man alone."

The girl searched the weapon room, checking in suits of armor and behind large shields to find the hidden wizard. All the while she held tight to the sword, telling herself it was for protection and not the desire for power.

"Stop fidgeting girl," ordered the wizard. His voice reverberated in the low-ceilinged room. "I'm a thousand leagues away and ten years in the past. You are in the moment. Put your mind at ease and listen to the sword."

Elyzabel abandoned her search. She stood in the middle of the room and closed her eyes. In a moment, she felt a growing heat from the sword. It surged up her arm and filled her heart. Then a new voice came to her. All at once, it sounded like the wizard and the owner of the sword, but also her own voice. And still, under that combined chorus, she heard a deeper, more powerful sound. The voices spoke in unison.

"Look to the sky. You must go when it comes."

Then the voices faded, and along with it that comforting warmth disappeared. Even the bright clarity diminished.

"Well?" asked the wizard. "What did it say?"

"It said I have to go somewhere," Elyzabel explained to the empty room. It seemed right to put the sword back in its resting place.

"You have been chosen," replied the wizard.

"For what?" asked Elyzabel. She wished she never touched the sword. She wanted to leave this room, but did not think she still wanted to go to the laboratory.

"How should I know," answered the wizard, "I'm not even there. And besides, it did not choose me. Why don't you go play with the telescope in my lab like you seem to enjoy. You might find some comfort there."

Elyzabel felt a little guilty that the wizard knew of her secret visits. She said *thank you* to the empty room, but could no longer feel the wizard's presence.

In the observatory above the lab, Elyzabel found her sense of wonder that always came with looking out at the unending stars. Her unease faded like the power from the sword. For a moment, she only felt the magnificence of space and time. Then something happened that changed her feelings.

A black object obscured the lens. It seemed to be coming straight towards her. She ran outside to watch the falling object with her naked eye. She saw it crash into the center of the courtyard. Thankfully, at this late hour, no one was hurt. Under the dark night sky and a few scattered torches that happened to stay lit, she could only tell it was a shiny black rock with peculiar silver speckles.

That night, after the commotion died out, she lay awake wondering if this was what the sword meant for her. *Was she supposed to go when this thing came? Where was she supposed to go?* Elyzabel could not sleep for fear of what might come next.

Over the next several days, many people investigated the rock. They even tried to move it, but with no success. Elyzabel felt uneasy until the wizard finally returned in his physical form. She met him in the courtyard, but did not get a chance to speak because she was interrupted by a massive hawk soaring over the golden wall.

Several knights drew their crossbows, but the wizard ordered them to hold.

The hawk spoke with what Elyzabel considered an odd accent. "I came across the plains to find this one maiden. She is needed with much importance."

The wizard turned to Elyzabel with a knowing smile. "I think this is what you've been waiting for my dear."

She knew in her heart that he was right, but she was not sure if she was ready to go.

"You will not go unprotected," said her cousin's husband. "I would give you my own sword, but in its stead, please accept this." The wise leader of these brave knights held up a short, thin blade that glistened black under the bright sun. "With great effort, I managed to cut a sliver of that strange stone with my magic blade. Nothing else could affect it. It is an effective weapon of which I hope you never have need."

Elyzabel examined the blade, almost as long as her arm. The slice of rock looked so thin, she thought she could almost see through it. The silver specks winked at her, dancing across the wavy blade. Holding it, she wondered why he chose to affix it to a smaller hilt than one better suited to a knight's larger hand. It was as if it had been designed solely for her.

"Thank you," she said, not sure she would know how to use a sword, if the time came.

Without further discussion, Elyzabel mounted the back of the great bird. Together, they sailed off to follow the sun across Empyrean.

Chapter 20

The First Queen of the Southern Valley

The southern people were first known as the children of the land. They grew from the animals of the desert and the river. As such, every animal is sacred and many southerners still bear a resemblance to their ancestors.

The people promptly developed skills as farmers on the fertile plains near the powerful Brygos River. They also learned to be artists and musicians, but more than that, they were builders. These skilled builders created an architectural marvel at the southern tip of the rich farmland and called it Hierakonpolis.

They designed the city to be the center of their great land. They planned huge monuments to their sacred animals and established a magnificent marketplace that took years to build.

One of the first temples to be completed was to honor the cow. These creatures provided food and milk. They also helped with labor on the farms. The cow-headed mother, Hathor, presided over this temple.

On the opposite side of the wide, dusty avenue, Hathor's cat-headed friend, Bastet, oversaw the shrine of cats. The southern people praised the hunting abilities of all cats, especially lions.

Hathor and Bastet met in the open courtyard to teach their magic to others. They accepted anyone that wanted to learn, young or old. One of their most promising students came to them at five years of age.

Through the naming ritual, her parents called her Shai. Hathor and Bastet knew the child's name meant *fate* and they could see she was fated to excel with magic.

Shai looked nothing like her teachers. While they had tall, strong bodies, barely covered to honor their powerful feminine forms, Shai remained small and skinny. At five years, she should already have shown signs of being strong like others in her family, but she did not. While she had dark skin, she did not tan like Bastet, whose skin matched the fur on her golden swaying tail. Shai had a human head, which had become more and more common with her people. Her short black hair curled around her shy face. She did not show the fierceness of Bastet, nor the strength of Hathor.

The one thing Shai shared with these two great women was her instant ability to use magic. Even being distracted, as a child can be, Shai learned faster and became more adept than the other adults that started learning before her. She could make water dance and lift heavy objects by pointing at them. She could communicate with the wild animals and whisper to someone across the room without moving her lips.

Many days, Hathor or Bastet would take Shai into their respective temples for private lessons. Over the next year, while Shai did not grow much in stature, she grew in power. Her meekness became humility and the people began to regard her as a sacred figure who might one day be their leader.

Because of this, on the day the black rock fell into the Southern Valley, she was among the first to inspect it.

Many people witnessed the rock drop from the sky. They saw it first over Nata Playa, the great lake, and it followed a course over the River of Life. When the rock hit the ground, it splashed into the Brygos. The mysterious rock smashed into the muddy river bed so hard that it bore deep into the ground. The fast-flowing river filled in the hole so fast that no one could say for certain how deep it went.

The engineers devised a plan to temporarily re-route the river. They all agreed that the life-giving Brygos should not be tainted by this rock. At the south end of town, they dug a tunnel that would carry the Brygos under all of Hierakonpolis. The river would not see sunlight again until it surfaced where the strange stone could not touch it. The digging, however, caused a cave in where the rock had crashed. The river trickled out of the newly formed entrance of a pitch black cavern. Ten grown men could stand shoulder to shoulder and barely reach each side. Throwing a lit torch into the maw did nothing to light the way.

Hathor, Bastet, Shai and their master snake charmer decided to enter the tunnel. With the help of three torches and a little magic, they could see the rock with its mystifying silver speckles about twenty paces into the tunnel.

The snake charmer looked around the dark cave. Shai noticed him shivering, but it was not cold. He said, "I fear this stone has opened the door to Abydos."

"What's Abydos?" asked Shai. It had not come up in her years of lessons. Apparently, Hathor and Bastet felt they needed to protect her from some things.

The gentle woman with the cow's head said, "Abydos is where our lost loved ones go for peace."

"Ha," stuttered the snake charmer. "It is no place for the living though."

Bastet hissed at the man. He stopped his stammering and moved quickly out of the cave. The others followed without further explanation of Abydos.

Once back in the warming sunlight, Shai asked, "What should we do about that stone?"

"We will do nothing," answered Bastet.

"The builders will finish the tunnel and it shall be drowned from our sight," added Hathor. "It has no purpose for us."

Shai felt uneasy. She said, "And what of Abydos?"

"Call it what you will," said Bastet, "once the mighty Brygos flows through there, the tunnel will be impassable. I believe it poses no harm to our crops or people from down there."

A farmer interrupted them. "Mistress Hathor, a thousand pardons. I went to your temple for you to bless my calf."

Hathor, with Bastet and Shai, followed the farmer to her temple only to find a full grown bull.

"Where is your calf?" asked Hathor.

The farmer looked embarrassed. He gestured to the black bull and said, "That is why I sought your blessing in person. He was born only yesterday."

Shai could not believe this strong black bull had lived only one day. She barely reached the bull's chest and she already passed eight years. "What's his name?" she asked.

"Such an exceptional beast, I had hoped he would be named here," said the farmer.

"Indeed," said Hathor. She partially knelt and partially bowed to put her head level with the bull. She turned her head so that their horns gently touched. After a moment of silence, Hathor said one word, "Apis."

After several days spent with Apis, Shai could feel a connection to him like no other animal she had known. Although he said almost nothing, she suspected he felt the same about her.

Hathor instructed the farmer to take Apis back to the fields for some time. She finished by saying, "His purpose will be with us soon."

A short time after the farmer left, a commotion drew much attention to the west side of Hierakonpolis. Four unidentifiable figures raced south toward the desert. Moments later, two more figures approached from the north. One continued on, apparently chasing the first four.

The one that stopped impressed Shai. He reminded her of Hathor and Bastet, except much taller and with the head of a regal hawk.

"Pardon the intrusion, but these are dire times," said the hawk man. "I am Horus."

Horus looked like he had long been in battle and needed rest. Shai decided to put a sleeping spell on him without discussing it first. To her, it seemed like a kind gesture. She did not realize the importance of his mission or even think that he might have something more to say to them.

By the time they had sleeping Horus carried to the Temple of the Wing, another great bird arrived. This giant hawk did not appear battle weary, but he looked intent, determined and in haste.

"I have come across the Central Plains in search of a powerful maiden. She is significantly needed," explained the hawk.

Bastet said, "I am certain this is connected to Horus and the fiends to which he gave chase."

"It may also have well to do with that mysterious rock," said Hathor. "You should go with this master bird, Shai. Have confidence in your abilities, they will serve you well."

Shai climbed on the hawk's back. She said, "I am ready, master bird."

As the hawk took wing, Bastet called after them, "Safe journey."

The girl and bird flew north into the blue of the sky.

Chapter 21

The First Queen of the Eastern Sky

Nyssa spent enough time in the goblin prison. She could not wait to get out into the fresh air, even if it made her light headed and giddy. When they made it to the surface, the bright light hurt her eyes. Aleria helped her find a seat on a nearby rock and Nyssa could already feel the mountains impairing her senses.

While the elves secretly worked on something by the cave entrance, the nightingale landed on Nyssa's shoulder.

"Thank you, dear friend," said Nyssa. "I know I've taken you out of your time, but we would still be trapped if not for you."

The nightingale gave a victorious trumpet. The sound must have attracted the attention of the others. The lead elf approached with a pointy-toothed smile. He said, "We have sealed that goblin cave such that no one will ever find it again." He gestured at the mechanical bird. "This is a brave and unusual friend you have here. He found us in the main pass, far below. We were sent by the tribal princesses to search for allies in the east. A war is coming."

"I thought so," said Nyssa.

Aleria asked Nyssa, "Is this about the black rock and everything you told me?"

"It has to be," said Nyssa. Then to the elf, "Are these princesses on the plains now? Are there giants with them?"

The elf looked somewhat surprised. He said, "There is one giant. We know him of old as Father Odin."

"Can you take me to him?" asked Nyssa.

"It is not our mission." The elf stopped and looked to his comrades. "However, I feel there is something unusual about you, as well. Although we have yet to gather an army, it may be best that we escort you there now."

"Oh wait," said Nyssa. She remembered the Prismata telling her to do something if she met any elves. She reached inside the pouch still slung at her hip to verify she still had the three crystals she took from Raymond Shaydaway. Then she handed the whole pouch to the lead elf. "I'm supposed to give these to you."

The elf looked inside the pouch. Without any other questions, he said, "I understand."

They decided to travel north along the mountain top. The elves felt it would be too dangerous for the girls trying to climb down the side of the cliff. The lead elf said there would be a bridge to take them over the mountain pass.

For quite a while, they walked along a narrow ledge. The girls laughed for no real reason. Nyssa could not tell how high they were because clouds filled the chasm. The one good thing about the Euphoric Mountains was that her fear of heights did not bother her. Some kind of energy definitely flowed from the mountains. It gave her a false sense of calm or maybe made her not care as much.

When they reached the bridge, Nyssa's mood faltered for a moment. The bridge turned out to be nothing more than two ropes stretched across the heart stopping drop. She guessed the thick one along the bottom to be for feet and the smaller rope at waist height to be for hands. She did not believe the rush from the mountains delivered enough power to keep her from being scared now.

The clouds hung about ten feet below the lip, which almost tricked her into believing it was not as high as it actually was. That helped Nyssa's twisting stomach, a little. Also, she could throw a rock and easily hit the other side. She guessed she could make it across rather fast. She would not have time to think about falling. The lead elf proved that to be the case. He shimmied across the rope with as much ease as walking on flat ground.

"I want to try," said Aleria. The girl turned into a snake. She wound her way across to the other side faster than the elf even. The nightingale followed, flitting through the air.

"That's not fair," Nyssa said with a laugh. She did not feel quite ready to attempt the crossing. Three other elves went ahead of her. No one spoke, as they were focused on their delicate footwork. Nyssa could hear a breeze whistling through the peaks. Other than that, she only heard the creak of the rope being stretched and strained.

The last elf stood behind her. Nyssa thought he looked insistent that it was her turn. She eased one foot onto the thick double-braided rope. She gripped the top rope so tightly that she could feel little splinters poking her hands. She closed her eyes before she put her second foot on the rope. She kept sliding her feet, hoping to bring them together. With each move of her back foot, the rope swayed. Nyssa moved her front foot further out to keep balance.

When she opened her eyes, Nyssa did not expect to be halfway across the bridge. The surprise caused her to shift her weight and the bottom rope swung out from under her. Both feet slipped off the rope and Nyssa tightened her hand hold on instinct. She dangled in mid-air.

"Hang on!" shouted Aleria.

On both sides, an elf leaned out over the edge, trying to steady the bottom rope and pull it back close to Nyssa's feet. Nyssa did not feel too worried. Somewhere in the back of her mind, she wanted to scream. However, the mountains overwhelmed her with a calm that took the lives of so many lost explorers. She simply hung with her arms wrapped around the top rope, waiting almost patiently for help. Finally, the elves wrestled the rope into place and Nyssa regained her footing.

"Thanks," she said with a chuckle.

Then the rope broke.

The thick rope beneath her feet unraveled with an audible snap and Nyssa plummeted into the clouds. She did not drop straight down however. She kept her grip on the top rope and swung toward the rock wall. She could not see anything among the clouds and hit the mountainside with an unexpected jolt. She reacted without thinking and let go of the rope to brace against the impact. She immediately started sliding down the rock face. Purple pebbles scrambled under her palms as she searched for a handhold. She managed to stop by wedging her left foot into a narrow crack. Pressed against the wall, from her precarious position, Nyssa could see the frayed end of the rope only a few feet above her.

Aleria's voice came out of the mist like she was calling for a lost pet, "Nyssa?"

"I'm down here," said Nyssa.

"No kidding," responded Aleria. "How far down?"

"I don't know," started Nyssa, then, "I can see the end of the rope, but can't reach it. Otherwise, I don't know."

Despite the washing euphoria, Nyssa did not like her current situation. She pressed her hands flat against the mostly smooth rock. If not for the crack occupied by the tip of her left shoe, who knows how far she would have fallen. Over to her right, farther from the rope, Nyssa spotted a wider crevice. She could not tell if it went all the way up to the top, but it looked wide enough for her whole body. With one lunge, Nyssa slid slightly down and to the right. She instantly knew she would miss her opening and closed her eyes. Instead of falling, she slammed into the crevice. She took the brunt of the short fall on her back and knew she would have a bruise later. Still, she admitted, it was better than the damage of falling all the way to the bottom, however far that was.

"Are you still there?" Nyssa called, her head a little clearer from the impact.

"I'm right here," returned Aleria through the cloud cover.

Nyssa examined the surrounding rock. It looked like she would have enough hand and foot holds to make it back to the top.

"I'm going to try to climb," started Nyssa. A searing pain inside her head kept her from explaining more. She said, "Oh no. Not now."

Aleria must have heard her and realized what was about to happen. She started screaming, "No, no, no!"

Then, Nyssa switched.

For the first time in a while, she switched alone.

Nyssa's will to keep from falling overpowered the urge to faint. This did not stop her head from hurting though. Nyssa wedged herself in her crevice, waiting for the pain to pass. It hurt so bad, she could not even bring herself to call out for Aleria. Unfortunately, no call came to her either. When Nyssa finally felt well enough to move, she climbed deliberately. She took great care in her hand and foot placement. She realized she probably took longer than she needed to, but she did not want to risk falling if another switch came over her.

Eventually, she made it above the clouds and then to the ledge where she last saw Aleria. Of course, she saw no one now, not even any sign of the rope bridge. She thought she either travelled so far back before the bridge was built or so far forward that it completely decayed. With no rainbow overhead, she guessed it felt forward.

A sense of loneliness pulled at her heart, but Nyssa chose not to let it affect her. The mountains likely helped her ignore it. She looked around at her overly quiet surroundings. She could only find one path that looked to head up to the peak of this section of the mountains. At the top of this path, Nyssa came to a fork. With the sun straight overhead, she could not tell which way the two new paths went. She guessed one to be north and the other west.

Nyssa reasoned a path to the west would lead her back to the cliffs, so she decided to go what she thought was north. This path continued to go up, and as it did, it twisted. With each turn, Nyssa could not see the path behind or in front of her. Eventually, she came out into a wide basin.

The rock here looked smoother than other places, almost as if it had intentionally been made into this giant bowl shape.

A strong gust of wind broke Nyssa's musing. It would swoosh, pause for a moment, and then swoosh again. Nyssa looked up to see what storm might be coming. A massive flying figure blocked the clear sky.

The enormous bat-like wings rushed wind at her as they folded inward. Almost as fast, they extended out, only to push another swoosh of air down at her. Nyssa immediately recognized the amazing, giant, purple creature.

The dragon landed, apparently displeased to find someone in its nest. It stood on its hind legs and let its wings fold so tightly to its body that they became almost invisible.

"May I help you?" came the deep resonating voice and Nyssa knew it was a male dragon and she remembered him.

Maybe it was the power of the mountains, but Nyssa felt no fear in talking to this mighty creature. She said, "I know you."

"Impossible," replied the dragon. "No one knows Evorin that is not already in his stomach."

Evorin lowered his head, as if to show how wide he could open his mouth. Nyssa guessed she could walk inside like an elevator. She realized, however, that this particular elevator only went down. She insisted, "No. I saw you at a village, talking to a bunch of animals."

The dragon twisted his lips into what Nyssa thought might be a smile. He said, "Then you are definitely wrong. I do not talk to animals. I eat them. And, I avoid the villages. *Now* is a dangerous time to be a dragon."

"I'm sorry, but I know what I saw. And I don't think it was *now*. I switch around a little. It might not have happened for you yet," she explained.

Evorin rose back up, only to drop onto all four legs. He circled the nest like a cat and found a comfortable spot to sleep.

He said with a yawn, "You have seen my future. This is something I do not take lightly. What is your name, child?"

"Nyssa."

"Ah," said Evorin. "That explains it. I will heed your words, although I have no plans of going to any village. This is a rare opportunity for a human to talk with a dragon, especially a human like you. Can I answer any questions or clarify any misconceptions?"

Before Nyssa could ask anything, she felt another painful switch starting. "Some other time," Nyssa said. Then her vision blurred.

Maybe it was the power of the mountains, but for the second time, Nyssa did not pass out when she switched. When her vision cleared, she expected to still be in Evorin's nest, but did not expect to see Evorin.

She immediately found out she was wrong. He looked bigger, but otherwise the same. He must be older, Nyssa reasoned. That meant she probably guessed wrong about being in the future last time. It was so hard to keep track for her. The dragon looked busy with other visitors and his tail blocked one of the two paths out of the nest. A man with shoulder length hair held out his sword, ready to use it. He looked to be considering whether it would be a good choice to strike. Instead, he charged at the opening and climbed part way up Evorin's tail to see the other side. With one shake, Evorin tossed the man back into the center of the nest. The man landed next to an impressive black stallion.

"Did they make it?" asked the horse with what seemed to be great concern.

"The girls should be safely down the mountain before nightfall," answered the man.

"Do not worry about the morsels," said Evorin. Nyssa felt his intent to follow them remained unspoken. "They solved my riddle and earned safe passage. It is yourselves that you should worry for now."

Evorin opened his mouth, revealing all of his frightening teeth. He lowered his head slowly, as he had done for Nyssa moments before. He did not look like he was going to stop before having his meal this time.

Then Nyssa recognized the man. He looked older, but it was the broken hearted William from the frozen forest.

She yelled, "Wait. Stop!"

All three turned to look at her. This made Nyssa momentarily uncomfortable.

"Where did she come from?" asked the horse. Something about him reminded her of the colt, Wrath, she met in the unicorn meadow.

"I hoped we would meet again," said Evorin. He instantly changed his demeanor from monster to friend.

"Humble thanks for your intervention," said the older William. It might have been a trick of the mountains, but Nyssa thought he looked younger now than when she first arrived in this moment.

"You should bow when you say that," suggested Evorin. "But of course, you do not know who this is."

Nyssa said, "I think I recognize them though. I'm pretty sure they were at the village with you when you talked to the animals."

The horse trotted closer to Nyssa. He said, "Hay, we know a village full of animals."

William said, "Fury, please, let the maiden speak."

Fury backed away and said, "Sorry, William."

Not really used to speaking in front of strangers, Nyssa looked at Evorin and he seemed to be expecting something from her. She spoke directly to the dragon. "I don't know. I think maybe you are supposed to help them. Maybe see what they need from that village?"

"It is fortune to see you so near the beginning," said Evorin. He looked pleased with himself. "To know you once lacked confidence and conviction is so unlike when I met you near the end. Still, your instincts are keen. I will see what they request."

Now this version of William looked embarrassed. He said, "At this point, the only thing that might help us is an army."

Evorin reared up on his hind legs and spread his wings wide. He said, "Then I do this as a favor from the last of my kind to the first of her kind. Let us go to this animal village and raise an army."

The horse, Fury, added, "We should see if the unicorns will join us too."

Nyssa did not get to hear any further discussion of unicorns or armies. Another switch came and this time, blackness came with it.

When Nyssa awoke, she could still feel the remnants of her headache. She looked around for Evorin, but his nest did not even look the same. Strewn with rocks, it had yet to be worn smooth. He must not live here yet, Nyssa guessed. She could not even find the second exit, so she had no choice but to return the way she came.

Nyssa followed the path back to the fork. She saw no point in returning to the bridge, so she took what she thought of as the west path. As she continued to gradually go up, the clouds seemed to get thicker. After several minutes, she could only see the path a few feet ahead and a few feet behind. She could no longer hear the wind and her own footsteps sounded muffled.

If Nyssa had not been looking at her feet, she would have walked off one of the highest cliffs in the chain of the Euphoric Mountains. The ground ended suddenly. She checked to her right and left to discover the path led her up a narrow outcropping, some kind of point. She only had the ground under her feet and the path behind with barely enough room to turn around without falling.

"This seems like a good spot to take a break," Nyssa said aloud to herself. At this height, her voice echoed among the clouds and distant rocks. She sat on the ledge and let her feet hang over the side. She thought of Aleria, Evorin, William, talking horses and unicorns.

A sense of peace overwhelmed Nyssa. At this moment, she felt completely alone, yet totally safe. Despite all she had lost and actually being lost, she felt like singing. She tried to remember the words to one of the old songs she wrote, but ended up adding new words to the tune.

> *From the ocean shores to the mountaintop*
> *Who has searched for me?*
> *If I were lost and alone*
> *Would you search for me?*
>
> *Walking through the woods with you*
> *Can you stay with me?*
> *Living all my life with you*
> *Will you stay with me?*
>
> *Sitting on the mountaintop*
> *With only clouds to see*
> *Now I am lost and alone*
> *Would you search for me?*

Somewhere in the world below
Together again some day
And then the dragon's wing
Will blow the clouds away

At first, Nyssa thought she heard clapping, as if someone applauded her song. Whatever it was, a rhythmic whooshing greeted the end of her words. Maybe Evorin found her, she hoped, but it sounded too small.

Through the clouds, a giant hawk appeared, not nearly as big as a dragon, but far larger than any bird she had ever seen, even the Prismatas' swan.

The hawk said, "If not for the beauty of your voice, I never would have found you. I left the Central Plains in search of someone like you and I think you have long been needed."

The giant bird hovered in front of Nyssa, its muscular wings continuously flapping. She felt a relief that she had not yet known in this strange, frightening land. She had been in danger. She discovered new friends. And lost them. At this moment, Nyssa felt something she had not felt in years. She felt hope. Finally, she believed, she neared the end of her journey.

Chapter 22

The First Preparations

If Nyssa thought she was near the end of her travels, she soon realized how wrong she was. The hawk carried her on his back down from the mountains. Before he broke through the clouds, he rose up high into the bright sunlight. The warmth caressed Nyssa's face.

Then they dove.

The hawk sailed down the side of the Euphoric Mountains and swooped out over a wide, grassy plain. He dropped low, almost close enough for his wings to touch the high reeds. Nyssa looked over the tall grasses that swayed in a never-ending breeze. It reminded her of the oceans and Banookanook, which felt so long ago.

The last time she felt the rush of wind in her hair like this had been when she first arrived in Empyrean. The blasts from Evorin were momentary, but this felt like it would never stop. She had been scared and confused, soaring on that shattered rock. Now, at least, she felt a little less of both. The sensation also reminded her of Gulfaxi. He was a fast horse, but his thunderous gallop did not ride as smooth at the flight of this hawk.

Nyssa felt herself relax with the breeze in her face. Thinking of Gulfaxi made her wonder in what time she left him. Because she came back to the goblin prison, she thought maybe she was close to the same time when she lost both the horse and girl. She did not want to hope she switched back to Aleria and simply missed her on the foggy path.

She tried to force the thoughts of her lost friend out of her head. She knew it would be too painful to hope to see the girl again. The chance of another meeting seemed impossible. Nyssa admitted she let herself get too close to Aleria, something she learned a long time ago not to do with people. Still, she had met the nightingale more than once.

"What if?" Nyssa whispered.

A thunderclap scattered her concerns like leaves blown from a sidewalk. An unexpected storm rose up in front of them.

"We will have to circle around to the south," said the hawk, his voice barely audible over the growing turbulence.

A wall of dark clouds stacked up to their right as they turned south. The hawk attempted to put more space between them and the storm. From their new height, Nyssa could see the storm ravaging the plains with lightning and torrents of rain.

Fortunately, in a short while, the storm became a dark spot on the horizon, its sudden danger forgotten. The altered course gave Nyssa something different to look at below and it did not make her feel any better.

Marching up from the south on her left, she saw a massive army spread across the plains, trampling the beautiful grasslands. Nyssa knew instantly that they were not friendly. She could feel their malice, even miles away. At first, she thought they were dinosaurs, but they walked on two legs like humans. These yellow-scaled creatures looked heavily armored and carried huge battle axes and clubs.

Even if Nyssa could not sense the monsters' palpable rage, she only had to look at the head of the army to know they were evil. She saw four unmistakable figures. Even in their first brief encounter, Nyssa would never forget the oily black giants that fought against Odin and his friends.

The hawk changed course again, putting the army behind them. They flew north at such a speed that Nyssa watched the army fade out of sight. The hawk flew with renewed purpose and flapped his powerful wings harder than seemed possible.

As they flew, the land gave way to a wide canyon. A powerful river flowed over the edge, cascading into a beautiful waterfall. Nyssa wondered if this was the same area where she first arrived in Empyrean. She knew there was no canyon though and whatever remained of the black rock should be right in the center of that massive hole.

When Nyssa saw the roiling, bubbling black mists deep in the canyon, she thought she understood. Nyssa guessed the shattering of the rock ripped open the ground and everything collapsed. She hoped the Forgotten Evil fell into that hole before it had a chance to escape. Maybe, she thought, this gave Odin a chance to stop the darkness. Then her mind slipped to a darker thought that Odin might not even be here and maybe there was nothing she could do on her own anyway.

As fast as they left the army of monsters behind, those negative thoughts left Nyssa. A new sight stretched across the plains north of the canyon. Almost as numerous as the dinosaurs, Nyssa saw an army of elves making preparations for war. She saw them training with spears and bows and swords. She saw countless tents that reminded her very much of Native American teepees. Many groups of elves gathered around recently lit bonfires, although the sun had not yet dipped out of sight in the east.

The hawk flew in low, directly over the center of the massive camp. Nyssa spotted their destination, a low tent, wider than the others. Sitting at the biggest of the campfires, in front of this tent, she recognized the unmistakable figure of Father Odin. He wore the same battle-torn rags, but to Nyssa, still had a peaceful resemblance to Santa Claus.

Odin stood as the hawk landed in the clearing. Two impressive female elves walked out of the main tent, as if on cue. They looked identical to Nyssa, except that one had blonde, almost white, hair and the other had midnight black hair, both down to their knees. Odin scooped Nyssa from the hawk's back like she remembered him scooping up that little girl back in Banookanook. Nyssa felt quite safe and comfortable and only a little self-conscious.

"I feared we lost you when the stone split," said Odin. He put her on the ground in front of the twin elves. He continued, "This is Malika," pointing to the dark haired woman first, and then to the blonde, "and Marika. They are the tribal princesses and heads of Clan Lantisphere. They have agreed to lead all of the clans with me against the Forgotten Evil and his army. You may call me Odin."

Nyssa realized, in this time, they had not been introduced. For him, it had probably only been a few days since she splashed into that river at his feet. She could only guess that their meeting in Banookanook took place hundreds of years in his future. After a moment, she recovered from that revelation and said, "My name's Nyssa."

"Nyssa the Traveler," said the dark elf Malika. "We have heard of you."

"From a prophecy?" guessed Nyssa.

"No," said Malika. "From your friend."

At first, Nyssa thought it was her imagination, then she realized Aleria actually walked out of the tent behind the twins. The force of emotion hit her as hard as the pain of switching. Both girls cried and buried their faces in hugs, squeezing so hard that they might never let go.

Nyssa could not bring herself to speak, but Aleria attempted her usual quirky attitude. With a sniffle, she said, "I knew you'd come back for me."

This sent the girls into another round of thankful tears.

Odin and the elves let them enjoy their reunion for a moment longer before the giant interrupted. He said, "I'm sorry, but we must discuss what is coming."

As they gathered in front of the large fire and waited for a few more elves to join them, Nyssa wanted to talk to her friend. "How did you get here?"

"After you fell, I knew that you switched," said Aleria. "Of course, we didn't know where you went. The elves still wanted to get down off the mountain. They don't like what the euphoria does to their senses."

"And they brought you here? I thought they were looking for an army," said Nyssa.

"Once they saw my ability, they decided to bring me straight back. We only got here this afternoon. There's some funny talk about needing some special girls and I guess I'm one of them," finished Aleria.

The gathered elves started talking in their own language. This gave Nyssa the opportunity for one more question. She hoped Aleria would have a good answer for her. She meant to ask about those crystals, but changed her mind at the last moment. "Did the nightingale come with you?"

Aleria looked saddened by this, but Nyssa thought she also looked a little hopeful. She said, "He went east. I think to look for you. I guess it will be a few years before he finds you though."

This news made Nyssa sad, but also happy that they would meet again in his future. She wished she had more time to share her music with the mechanical bird. It seemed now that they would never have another chance.

"But good news! Gulfaxi is here," added Aleria. "Odin is going to ride him into battle. I'd say that's exciting. And terrifying."

"He found his way across the plains? That is good news," said Nyssa. One less friend no longer lost to time gave her some relief.

Malika stood. The elves finished their debate and the elven princess looked ready to talk to the girls. She said, "The old father told us the dire story of the loss of balance in the world. Empyrean is new to this world and humans are new to Empyrean. An army comes to raise a Forgotten Evil. For the sake of all beings, we will fight the First War for Empyrean."

Nyssa did not like the idea of going to war, but it was unavoidable now. Somehow, after everything she had gone through, however, she felt ready for it. Empyrean started to feel more real than her old life. She felt at home here, although she did not even have her own bed.

Malika looked deep into Nyssa's eyes, as if she was reading her mind. "Child, do not be too hasty to fight. You have something more to do, although I do not know what. As you said, there is a prophecy. That four maidens shall stand at the brink to deliver what was forgotten. Until these dark days, yet we do not fully understand, those words had no meaning to our people."

"The brink could be the edge of the canyon," guessed Nyssa.

Odin offered, "That was my thought as well."

"But there are only two of us," said Aleria.

"What?" said Nyssa.

"Two maidens. Me and you. Didn't she say there are supposed to be four?" asked Aleria.

"As one of the great hawks found you, Traveler, so have other hawks been dispatched in search of the chosen ones," explained Malika.

"I could be one of the chosen ones," said Aleria. Nyssa thought her friend looked eager. However, the elves did not look as encouraging.

"It is not for you young one. Your path lies in a different direction. For now, stay close to your friend," said Malika.

Aleria looked defeated, her mood changing from elated to hurt. She pointed at Marika, who had not said a word during their entire conversation. Aleria said, "What about her? What does she say about it?"

"My sister does not speak, but we are of the same mind," said Malika. "Her voice is a destructive force. One of our greatest weapons. Beyond that, we are ever in agreement. It is no slight to you, young one. You are the constant companion of the Traveler and your place is at her side."

"You're right about that at least. I have to stay close to her from now on, in case she switches again," said Aleria.

"Switches?" asked Odin.

"Yes. That's what we call it. I switch times uncontrollably," said Nyssa. She tried to remember how Odin explained it to her back on the beach. "It's a problem of, um, stability. I seem to have lost my, what'd you call it? Anchor? I guess I got too close to that black rock and absorbed some bad energy. The real problem is how bad it hurts when I switch and I think it's getting worse."

Malika put her hand under Nyssa's chin and raised her head, turning it side to side. "You seem to be afflicted with a unique ailment. We may have something that will help you. Elven medicines are quite powerful and have their own uniqueness."

The silent elf left the circle and returned after a moment with a small glass vial. Marika handed it to Nyssa.

Malika nodded to her sister, then explained, "Drink the potion. It will burn up the bad magic inside of you. Your untethered problem may get worse for a short time, but the pain will be gone at once."

Nyssa had no reason not to trust the elf or her potion. It tasted bitter, but Nyssa did not feel any different. She whispered to Aleria, "Hold my hand in case this stuff didn't work."

Another elf seated at the fire, that looked like an Eskimo to Nyssa, said, "I think we should turn our attention to the matter at hand."

"Frigent Algis, I hear your words, but all things must be in order," said Malika.

The male elf looked offended. He stood to address Malika. "I ask your pardon, but we have come down from the frozen north. Even the Rontogu clan has come from the far waters. For what? To aid some humans? This is the largest gathering of clans since your father passed into the twilight. The Immortals have bestowed many gifts on us. Now is a time for action to show our thankfulness, even if it is to save humans."

Now Odin took a turn to speak. He said, "Friend, your sacrifice will not be in vain. If you are ready for action, please tell me how you will stand against ten thousand Carcharodans led by the legendary General Bleog?"

"I know nothing of this Bleog and his Carcharodans and I fear them even less," said Frigent. He sat down without another word.

Odin spoke to all of the clan leaders. "We will not only face the four scarred and twisted lieutenants of the Forgotten Evil. They have gathered their army from Arcenland in the far south. The Carcharodans stand nearly as tall as myself, but they are vicious with tooth, claw and tail."

Nyssa surmised he was talking about the dinosaur creatures she saw earlier that day.

He continued, "Their general may be among the shortest of his race, but he is the most vicious. Bleog is a master strategist, but also a beast without compassion. He will drive his army down upon you with no concern for his own casualties."

"We have gathered, at most, six thousand," said Malika.

"Maybe we can help with that," came a woman's voice from outside the circle.

Everyone looked around, but saw no one. Nyssa thought she recognized the voice, but she could not say for sure until she spotted the tiny woman hovering above the group. Her small butterfly wings beat rapidly and her red dress glistened in the firelight.

"Ruby!" exclaimed Nyssa.

"I am she and these are my sisters, the Prismata," said Ruby.

Five other fairies joined Ruby, fluttering over the heads of the elves.

Ruby continued, "We are not like other fairies. We have some good magic to share. I know elves are skilled with the bow, but we can help ensure that every arrow flies true. If any lack confidence, we can offer clarity of mind."

Nyssa asked, "What about Evorin? Can you bring the dragon to help?"

Lilac, the purple fairy, flitted over to Nyssa. She said, "My dear, dragons do not yet exist in

Empyrean. I promise I will remember Evorin's name for when he is needed in the future yet to come."

Malika spoke to Ruby with respect, "Prismata, we graciously accept your offer of assistance."

"You surely will be rewarded," added Odin.

Ruby and her sisters floated up higher into the night air. She said, "We do not ask for a reward, only for the peace that should follow."

Then the Prismata flew across the camp, sprinkling their gold fairy dust on the elves as they settled in for their last good night of sleep. It tickled Nyssa's cheeks and made Aleria sneeze. The sudden action turned her into a butterfly and instantly back to human.

Malika watched the girls out of the corner of her eye. She seemed to resist a smile and then spoke to the northern elf. "Frigent Algis, have you anything now to add?"

The elf looked like he had renewed confidence. He said, "We should march out to meet the enemy before they come for us."

"I agree," said Odin. "If we are at the pit before the Carcharodans, we may gain some unforeseeable advantage."

The other clan leaders agreed in their own language. After a short night of solid sleep, six thousand elves marched across the Central Plains. Odin, riding Gulfaxi, led the way. Nyssa, holding tightly to Aleria, walked with Malika and Marika Lantisphere. Overhead, the Prismata continued to dust them with magic. Far above them, the great predator hawks soared with a watchful eye.

After a short march, the leaders of this army stood at the northern edge of the canyon. Far, far down below, something seethed in the black mists. Nyssa recalled those tentacles. She thought she could see them lashing out of the depths and had no desire to see the body that controlled them. The stoic elven army waited in complete silence.

Then the sound of thunder filled the air. Except, it was not thunder. No storm clouds obscured the sky. Nyssa mistook the stomping of the Carcharodans as a coming storm. In a way, though, she was right.

Far on the southern horizon, Nyssa could make out the four frightening lieutenants leading their evil army. Before she could clearly make out the shapes of the orange-scaled monsters, her vision went blurry. At least, she told herself, she did not have the accompanying headache this time.

Nyssa squeezed Aleria's hand. She said, "Hang on."

Chapter 23

The First Friend, Again

A
pparently, the elven medicine did not fully work. While she felt no pain this time, Nyssa still was not cured. Then she remembered that Malika said her problem might get worse before it gets better. She wanted the switching to stop completely. Even without the headaches or upset stomach, she did not know how much more emotional pain she could take. Then Nyssa felt Aleria's hand in hers. It gave her so much relief to have her friend with her now, whenever *now* was.

Nyssa scanned their surroundings. They stood at the edge of the same canyon on the same grassy plains. Behind her, the ground had been destroyed. It looked like the aftermath of an earthquake. The ground rose up creating high walls on both sides that left them in a wide, isolated field. Strewn across the field, Nyssa saw enormous broken statues that reminded her of the Carcharodans. They lay discarded like a giant child's toys, forgotten and broken. Some were only heads. Nyssa's first thought of abandoned junk changed to the idea that this was some kind of monument to a battle from long ago. She did not think it was from the fight she left moments ago, but from some other time after that. The way the grass and moss grew up and around the weathered stone made the hair on the back of her neck stand eerily.

"I never thought I would see it in person," said Aleria.

Nyssa thought she meant the battle field, but her young friend stared up into the sky behind them. She followed Aleria's gaze to the center of the canyon. Piercing the overcast sky, the tallest tower Nyssa had ever seen jutted out of the canyon wall. She knew it had to be taller than any of the buildings in her previous home world. She had no real frame of reference, but guessed it to be over two hundred stories high.

From this distance, it looked like a magnificent tree. About halfway up and higher, smaller towers sprouted from the sides, stretching up toward the sky. Nyssa knew it was not a tree though, because it seemed to be made entirely of crystal and it hung out over the pit, growing from the side of the canyon.

"That's Castle Empyrean," said Aleria in awe.

"It's amazing," responded Nyssa, equally as reverent. She looked around and saw no one near. The place seemed to be abandoned and she did not like being in this unsettling graveyard, or battlefield, or whatever it was. "Do you think we can get inside?"

"I've always wanted to. We're going to have to circle the canyon. There is only one way in from the stories I've heard," said Aleria.

The girls took off at a steady pace, like they were taking a leisurely hike. Nyssa watched the gentle breeze push through Aleria's white hair and let it cool her own face. The walk took the better part of the day. Nyssa felt they could have been faster, but they were very careful not to get too close to the edge.

When they made it around to the front side of the crystal tower, a massive wall of thorns and briars blocked their path.

"What a waste of time," exclaimed Nyssa.

Aleria ran up ahead out of Nyssa's grasp. She said, "No it wasn't. There's an opening."

Nyssa caught up to her friend, grabbing her hand before inspecting a wide path cut into the brambles. Someone must have spent a long time hacking and burning their way through this tangled defense, thought Nyssa. The opening was wider than it was tall and the hewn limbs looked rotted. Nyssa ushered Aleria through the deadly thorns, not wanting to be outside of this increasingly sad place.

On the other side, they found a bridge that extended from solid ground to the one and only castle gate. Before running across it, Nyssa looked up at the tower again. This close, it gave her a different feeling than her previous astonishment.

The castle seemed to be alive. She did not think it felt healthy though. The walls seemed dull instead of shiny and reflective like a crystal should. In the courtyard, debris covered the ground and the stable look long unused. The castle seemed alive, but dying.

"This has to be the way," said Aleria. She climbed several steps, pulling Nyssa with her, to an open set of double-doors. It looked especially dark inside to Nyssa.

"I have a bad feeling about this," she said.

Aleria changed into a white rabbit and sniffed the air. She changed back and teased, "It smells safe, so you better come with me because I'm going in. You wouldn't want to switch and leave me here all alone."

Nyssa did not like being guilted into it, but she trusted Aleria's senses. She truly did not want to leave her friend in such a lonely place.

Inside, the castle did not seem to be in any better condition. The halls looked dim and something scratched deep gouges into the once smooth walls. Neither girl paid attention to their randomly changing course. They turned corners and climbed stairs without a thought of looking behind them.

When Nyssa finally looked back, something struck her as odd. She knew they had topped a narrow flight of stairs, yet somehow they now stood at the bottom of a wide, curving stair case. She could not make sense of it and tried to dismiss it as confusion from being in a dark, unfamiliar place. They continued down the hall and around a corner. Nyssa looked back for the staircase, only to be greeted by a solid wall where they was none a moment ago.

"Something's going on," said Nyssa.

Aleria examined the wall. "It's always magic with you. This must be some sort of enchantment."

Neither girl discussed it further, but they silently agreed to hasten their pace. They had no idea of what they were looking for or where they were going. The faster the halls changed behind them, the faster they moved, until they were outright running.

They stopped, out of breath, in a small room that offered them two directions to continue. One way led to a partially open door. The other appeared to lead outside. Nyssa took a breath to calm her nerves. It seemed, to her, that the castle itself conspired to lead them to this point. The natural sunlight drew Nyssa out of the gloom. They crossed the threshold together to find themselves on a small balcony. Far below, Nyssa could make out the debris covered courtyard. The fresh air felt good in her lungs, but without the euphoria of the mountains, the height made her dizzy. Still, she thought, it was better than the stale air inside the castle.

"Let's try the other way," suggested Aleria. "I don't think this is a good way to get back down."

Nyssa looked over the rail. Even with the few outcroppings and cracks, it would definitely be a fall as opposed to a downward climb. Surely, she believed, they could find their way out. Eventually.

They stepped back through the small room and pushed open the partially closed door. The boy standing there caused Nyssa to let out a small gasp.

"Who are you?" she asked.

"Does it matter to you?" he rudely replied.

Nyssa did not get a friendly feeling from this boy. Although he had pale white skin, he seemed dark in spirit. She guessed him to be about fourteen, but the dark circles under his bright blue eyes made him seem much older. He pushed a hand through his short brown hair and Nyssa could feel him staring through them, as if he was staring into their souls. She felt if she looked too long into his eyes that she would see the damage that made him seem so dark. That was not something she wanted to see right now.

"I'm Aleria and this is Nyssa. Please tell us your name?" said Aleria. Nyssa liked that even in these uncomfortable moments, Aleria tried to be friends with everyone.

"Call me Adam Mulgart," the boy relented.

Nyssa looked at his ragged clothing. She suspected he had been lost in this dreary place for a long while. She did not think he would be too willing to help, but she asked, "Can you get us out of here?"

Adam smirked at her request. He said, "I can absolutely do that. That's why I'm here. *She* told me you might be coming."

"She who?" asked Nyssa. The boy's words seemed less helpful and more ominous. She racked her brain to think which *she* Adam meant. Malika? Ruby? Who could even possibly know they were here?

"It doesn't matter," answered Adam. "She's gone now."

Aleria said, "Maybe we can help you? We can work together."

"You don't understand. There's a way out right over there." Adam pointed across the room to the balcony. Then he charged at Nyssa, screaming with redness welling up in his eyes.

Nyssa had no time to react.

A moment before Adam hit her, Aleria tackled the dirty boy.

She spun on her tiptoes and turned his bigger size against him.

The boy's weight advantage over both girls now propelled him toward the balcony rail uncontrollably.

At the last instant, Adam managed to snag Aleria's wrist.

They both toppled over the railing.

"No!" screamed Nyssa. Her heart ached at losing Aleria again.

She rushed to the balcony to see if she could help the girl that, only seconds before, saved her from Adam's rage. Looking down, Nyssa could not see anything as her eyes blurred with tears.

Then she switched.

Chapter 24

The First Meeting

"That's horrible," cried Olena.

"That's what is in the book," said Tym. Zandria thought he looked apologetic, but otherwise unsure of how to comfort her younger sister.

Dew said, "That can't be right. She gets her best friend back only to lose her a few pages later? What kind of story is this? Does it at least say what happens to the little animal girl?"

Tym answered, "I'm sorry, but it doesn't. I do not believe Nyssa ever saw Aleria again after she fell."

"She was pushed," corrected Zandria.

Ovara got up from her seat. She had a far off look in her eyes as she said, "Who was that boy? He seems...interesting."

"He seems terrible," said Olena. Then she added, "Sorry Adam," to the boy sitting across from her.

"I suspect that event happened some time in the future based on the description of the castle. I do not know of a time previously that it has seen such despair. I do not think we will ever have to worry about him," said Tym. "Maybe it will not come to pass at all, as I hope to never see Castle Empyrean in such a fallen state."

"Yes, but he said his name was Adam," said Ovara. She looked directly at their Adam. Zandria thought he seemed offended and defensive.

He did not hesitate to say, "The book specifically says he has brown hair. Mine's copper."

"And it always will be," added Olena and she almost giggled.

Zandria looked at her sister with that half smile and wondered how Olena knew that about Adam. She decided it was queen's intuition.

"What does it say his full name is again?" Adam asked Tym.

"Adam Mulgart," said Tym after checking the book.

Adam seemed to be getting at something. Zandria wanted to know what he was thinking. She went to him and led him to a quiet corner of the room. The others started chatting about the elves and Carcharodans.

"What is it?" asked Zandria.

"I knew somebody named Mulgart," said Adam. He looked distant, like he was trying to remember something.

"Do you know this boy? Is he dangerous?" pried Zandria.

"If he is who I think he is, he's not dangerous right now because he's only a toddler," said Adam.

This bothered Zandria. She considered if the boy actually existed in her time, would he be able to hurt her friends as well?

"I met a woman and her baby when I followed you across the Wasteland," continued Adam. "I basically saved their lives. Her name was Lady Mulgart, but she had not yet named the baby. I never thought she would give him my name."

Zandria countered, "If he even is the one and same."

Adam still held onto that distant look. "It is. The one thing that I've learned from this story is that there are no such things as coincidences when it comes to the queens and the Deep Magic."

"I don't like it," said Zandria. "That means something bad could happen to Castle Empyrean in only a few years."

After this deliberation, Zandria and Adam returned to the group. The talk turned from the impending battle to dessert. When Tym offered to read about the First Queen, they all skipped dessert except for Eisenhahn. Now seemed to be the appropriate time to revisit the topic of sweets.

"I like cake," announced the big iron man.

Tym apparently took that as a cue. He used a short strip of cloth to mark their page and closed the book. They left as a group with Zandria and Olena in the rear.

Olena whispered to her sister, "Something is bothering me."

This seemed to be something Olena did not want to share with the others. Zandria slowed her pace to give them some distance from the group.

"I know," said Zandria. "Everything seems to be going so wrong for that girl."

Olena clicker her tongue against her teeth, an old habit that sometimes showed her exasperation. "Not that. It's the thing that boy said."

"What was it?" asked Zandria. She stopped walking to concentrate on the words.

"He said *she told me you might be coming.* Who is *she*, Zan?" asked Olena.

The idea sent a chill down Zandria's back. It even made the little hairs on her arms tingle. *Who is she?* If the boy already existed, then this other person might already be here too. Zandria considered it for a moment. When she looked up from her sister's worried face, the rest of the group had turned the corner.

She thought they could catch up to them before the hallway changed, so Zandria grabbed Olena's hand. She pulled the young queen, running around the corner. That faint whisper of the Bell Chamber in her heart told Zandria it was already too late.

When they made the turn, instead of finding their friends, they found a surprise. Zandria slammed into a girl, who had been running toward them. Both she and the slightly older stranger toppled to the ground on their backsides.

"Ka!" shouted Olena. She expressed Zandria's shock.

Zandria got up without injury and offered her hand to the stranger. The girl had long, wavy, light brown hair. She and Zandria were about the same height, but the new girl clearly looked older. She dressed in a strange style that looked like something Dew might wear. Her footwear looked the most unusual to Zandria. The coverings did not seem to be boots, but the laces were not quite those of sandals. It suddenly dawned on Zandria who this girl had to be.

"Who are you?" demanded the stranger.

Without hesitation, Zandria answered, "I am Zandria of Banookanook and this is my sister Olena, Queen of the Eastern Sky."

"But I thought Remina was the queen," said the girl.

"She was. Before me," said Olena starting to smile. Zandria guessed her sister now knew the stranger too.

"You're not going to hurt me are you?" pleaded the girl.

"Of course not," said Zandria. "I think we know, but you haven't told us your name."

"I'm Nyssa."

Olena's smile beamed into a huge grin at hearing her name. She hugged Nyssa tightly. She said, "I've been so worried about you."

When Nyssa could pull herself from Olena's grasp, she asked, "What is she talking about?"

Zandria stepped between Olena and Nyssa. She did not want her sister touching the girl if she unexpectedly switched again.

"It's complicated," started Zandria. "We are reading your story."

"My story?" said Nyssa, looking confused.

"Yes. But I don't know where this part fits into it. Maybe we haven't read that far yet," said Zandria. She thought about it for a moment, then said, "It would probably be better if you left this part out altogether. It might confuse a lot of people."

"It's definitely confusing me," said Nyssa.

"Don't worry. It will make more sense later," consoled Olena.

Nyssa looked ready to run again. Zandria tried to calm her. She said, "I've learned you have to have confidence in yourself. We know things are going to be all right, but you have to believe it too."

Now Zandria thought the girl looked on the verge of tears. She guessed the incident on the balcony must have only happened moments ago from Nyssa's perspective.

"Maybe this will help?" suggested Olena. "I know some words that are very powerful. Even if you can't use them, maybe they'll make you feel better. You have to promise to remember them."

"I promise," laughed Nyssa, blocking the first of her tears. Zandria smiled too. Somehow her sister always knew what to say. And it seemed especially amusing for the younger girl to be making the older girl promise anything.

Olena whispered Snow White's incantation to Nyssa. Zandria recalled the old queen whispering similar words to Olena once upon a time.

"If we can find Tym, we can help you get out..." began Zandria. Nyssa's abrupt disappearance cut off the last of her words.

"She switched," said Olena, clapping as if she witnessed a delightful magic trick.

Then Tym poked his head around the corner. He said, "There you two are. If you'd like to join us for some cake, we have a battle to get to."

Chapter 25

The First War for Empyrean

Marika Lantisphere learned her ability at an early age, which meant she learned to stay quiet. She did not want to hurt anyone with her voice.

Other elves could use their voices to bend trees or part tall grasses. None had ever been as powerful as Marika. When she was a baby, she ruined more than one tent crying like babies normally do. For her safety and others, they left her out of many childhood games. Marika grew up isolated, but she was never alone.

She had Malika.

Her twin sister always stood by her side. If Marika was left out of a game or party, Malika would not join either. They spent their time in the forests or wandering the plains. They developed an unspoken language. Malika knew exactly what Marika was thinking with the slightest gesture. The dark haired sister would speak for both of them, especially at tribal gatherings and ceremonies.

They developed other skills, as well. Both became masters of the long bow. Malika's incredible eyesight allowed her to pinpoint targets hundreds of feet away. In fact, her eyesight became so powerful that she could see into the future often with great clarity.

They trained Marika's voice so precisely that she could extinguish a flame from one hundred feet away or strip one leaf from a blooming tree with a single sound. Predicting the leaf's path, Malika would then loose an arrow and nail the leaf to the tree before it hit the ground.

When they became the tribal princesses, Marika knew everyone would think Malika was solely in charge. What they did not understand was their secret language that allowed them to equally share every decision. When Nyssa the Traveler stood before them, the choice to go to war was not as easy as they thought.

Marika knew her sister envisioned the need for four girls, but she felt they could not wait. Mostly, the elves were a peaceful people. Before the clans settled in Empyrean, they had fought a few battles against other races, some amongst themselves. Some clans, like the Rontogu, fought better with swords. Marika's own family, the Lantisphere Clan, were hunters who preferred bows and knives. The Algis Clan proudly carried their great spears.

The old father, Odin, promised the elves many things in their dealings with him. It is believed that he gave the elves their strength and special abilities. If they went to war with him this time, he promised to share his life force. He said the elves would not gain immortality, but after this, they would live long, peaceful lives. Malika had foreseen the war and believed there would be a time of peace after it, but she also believed that everything came to a natural end. The sisters, together of course, decided to accept Odin's gift. They knew they would have to fight regardless, so it seemed right for their people to gain something.

Standing at the edge of the newly formed canyon, they waited for battle. Malika watched the far side, anticipating the Carcharodan army. Nearly six thousand elves from almost forty different clans seemed to be a magnificent army. The hundred additional giant hawks overhead only added to their might. Marika and her sister stood at the front of this spectacle with an Immortal riding a giant horse and the two strange girls.

The younger, white haired girl had an ability that almost made Marika jealous. She loved animals and wondered what it would be like to turn into any one of them. The other girl, the Traveler, seemed so different. Malika told Marika that she had a vision about her and that she would not stay rooted in one time for too long. Marika concocted a medicine for Nyssa's problem days before their meeting. When Nyssa and Aleria disappeared at this critical moment, she knew her medicine was not entirely effective yet.

Marika attracted her sister's attention to show that the girls had vanished.

"Too late. They're here," said Malika. She pointed to the opposite side of the canyon.

The mass and might of the Carcharodan army made Marika feel small. In that moment, six thousand elves did not seem nearly enough.

"For Empyrean," yelled Odin. He urged Gulfaxi forward and the pair of giants rounded the canyon edge. The elves raised their weapons with yells and war cries. The usually peaceful people rushed after Odin, flooding around both sides of the wide canyon to meet the dark forces.

The Lantisphere Clan remained in place. Malika had instructed them to keep their distance and use their bows because no other clan matched their skill. The strong archers began firing shot after shot. The arrows sailed high over the canyon and rained down on the Carcharodans. Malika, with her extraordinary aim, struck one of the black lieutenants. The arrow pierced deep into its scarred skin. The oily giant snapped off the shaft of the arrow, leaving the poisoned tip embedded. The beast showed no more sign of pain than being stung by a bee. It did not even slow its pace.

Both branches of their army raced around the sides of the canyon until they clashed with their attackers. When the opposing forces collided, Marika saw that the shortest Carcharodans were at least two feet taller than the tallest elves and numbered thousands more. Her heart sank as she realized most of the monsters stood around four feet taller than most of her kind. The difference in size and number drove a creeping sense of hopelessness into her heart.

The Carcharodan General Bleog swung a horribly vicious axe that knocked down elves as if he were cutting grass. In the first clash, only one of the evil army fell for every five elves lost. Marika watched Odin charge directly toward the black giants. The four of them pulled him from Gulfaxi and then they sank into the sea of Carcharodans.

Marika felt a slight tremor under her feet. She looked into the canyon to see the mists growing darker and higher. She also thought she saw tentacles flailing, but she would need her sister to confirm something at that far of a depth.

"Keep firing," demanded Malika.

Her sister's firm command shook some of the fear away for Marika and the rest of her clan. She and her sister almost never spoke to each other aloud. This surprised Marika. She notched another arrow and let it fly.

Now she could see her great tribe turning the tide, at least, a little. The Algis Clan led the left flank and the Rontogu pressed forward on the right. Instead of two forces smashing into each other, the battle seemed more convoluted and swirled. Marika could see elves cutting their way into the enemy so far that they now completely encircled the canyon.

On her side, she could see small packs of Carcharodans slowly working their way closer to the archers. Marika did not like the idea of being surrounded. Soon, it did not matter as the battle covered the Central Plains with the impossibly deep canyon at its center, like a whirlpool waiting to suck in its victims.

It seemed to Marika that their advantage came from the hawks' assault. The great birds flew wide and attacked from the rear. Although it took two hawks to lift one of the enemy, they did plenty of pecking and scratching along the way.

"Bleog is moving up the right side," said Malika. "I see him coming straight for us. He will expect us to retreat, but that is not what we will do."

Marika nodded in agreement. Malika instructed the archers to hold their ground at any cost and then the twins dashed into the fray.

The Carcharodans certainly had the size advantage, but they lumbered. The nimble elves easily dodged the huge serrated swords. The creatures' tails moved faster, but without precision. As she slipped through the crowd with her sister, Marika twisted and flipped, careful not to receive a single scratch. Malika matched her pace, side by side, using the same acrobatic skill to reach General Bleog before he knew they were there.

His massive axe knocked away several Rontogu directly in front of her. Marika tucked, rolled, grabbed an elven sword from the ground and blocked the axe on its backswing, inches from her head. She looked up the length of the handle, up the muscular arms and directly into the pointed snout of the Carcharodan General.

Bleog lashed his tail, clearing a few more elves. Malika did an aerial cartwheel over a second strike of his tail. The General hesitated for a confused moment as the Lantisphere twins prepared for their own attack. Seeing him so much smaller than his soldiers gave Marika some huge relief. He actually was only about a head taller than her.

"General," said a confident Malika, "it is time for you to surrender."

"Surrender to you?" asked the stunned General. He continued, "Do you know who I am?"

Marika looked around to discover, for some reason, no one else came close to them. The fighting on all sides left the three of them in a small open space.

Malika answered, "Do I know you? Only your name and that's more than I care to. I would say you are the runt of the litter though."

This enraged General Bleog. He rushed at them, swinging his axe sideways as if he wanted to cut them in half.

Malika split her legs to drop to the ground and Marika back flipped. The wide blade touched neither of them. Now both armed with swords, the sisters attacked Bleog. The General could barely defend himself form the constant flurry of strikes. He had no opportunity to return a single blow with his axe. Bleog now only used it as a shield.

At one point, Marika moved too far to Bleog's right. He managed to snap at her with his tail. It left a gash in her thigh that drove her to the ground on one knee. Before he could strike again, her sister sliced off the tip of his tail. Bleog pounced on Malika for that.

Head swimming, Marika tried to regain her focus. Bleog's powerful tail cut her deep on the outside of her thigh. Pain filled her body and tears welled in her eyes. She knew her sister struggled with Bleog on the ground, but she felt like she could not even move. From a short, but impossible distance, she watched Malika block his gnashing jaws with the broad side of her sword.

Over Bleog's back, Marika noticed the continuous zip of arrows. She looked back to see the rest of her clan remained untouched and this gave her new resolve. She understood that if the Lantisphere archers could still fire arrows that the Carcharodans were no longer advancing. Marika slowly stood with the help of her sword, now intent only on Bleog and her sister.

The clamor of the ongoing battle pressed in on them. They were losing their personal fighting space. Marika grabbed Malika by the ankle and pulled her out from under the General. Bleog let out a whelp as if he did not know what happened.

Marika looked again for the arrows. This time, she saw something different over the canyon. Out in the center, she watched Nyssa appear in mid-air. The girl instantly dropped into the pit. This made Marika want to scream and that gave her an idea.

The blonde haired twin started leading her sister toward the outer edge of the battlefield. Once clear of the fighting, they moved away faster. Marika looked back to see Bleog chasing them, as she hoped he would. Countless Carcharodans followed their leader until they left many of the elves behind.

The Lantisphere twins instinctively stood back to back, awaiting their attackers. At the front of the approaching horde, General Bleog raised his menacing axe.

Marika inhaled.

The moment before his axe came down, Marika shouted two words.

"BE GONE!"

She used her voice with all of the strength and concentration she could manage.

General Bleog and almost forty of the nearest enemy soldiers disintegrated in the shockwave. Another hundred or so flew backwards through the air. Another wave simply toppled to the ground from the sheer force of her voice. Marika noticed that she managed to drop her own clan's arrows from the sky. She knew she did not end the battle, but she hoped losing their general would break the army's spirit. To her disappointment, the beasts seemed to rally and gathered around the four horrid, smoky lieutenants.

The battle continued.

Chapter 26

The First Secret

Nyssa wanted to spend more time with Zandria and Olena. They reminded Nyssa of her and Aleria. They also seemed to have a lot of answers to questions she did not know she had. Plus, they were going to show her how to get out of the castle maze.

Unfortunately, her blurring vision told Nyssa that their encounter was at an end. The switch happened in the middle of Zandria's sentence. Nyssa did not even get to say goodbye, but *what's new* she thought.

The instant change from the dark, narrow hallways to the bright, open air almost overwhelmed Nyssa. An arrow flashed in front of face, then she was falling. Nyssa's mind raced. How could she be falling? Panic took hold and she could not even inhale enough to scream. Spinning wildly, she could barely tell that she was over the middle of the canyon and dropping toward its depths. Somehow, her mind rationed that she switched back to a time before the castle existed and it made some kind of sense.

As Nyssa plummeted toward the churning black mists, her mind played tricks on her. She knew no one could catch her. The momentary glimpse of the elves told her they were too busy fighting to possibly even notice her, let alone attempt a rescue. Dropping closer to the mists, Nyssa's thoughts turned from hitting solid ground to being entangled in one of those tentacles. All of these thoughts passed instantly through her head, but her whole life did not flash before her eyes. She could not decide if that was disappointing or not. She drew rapidly closer to those dark tentacles struggling to pull the rest of itself out of the canyon. She decided it would be far better to smash into some jagged rocks than being caught by the Forgotten Evil.

For the first time, Nyssa wished for a switch. They always seemed to come at an unwanted time. *Why not now?* Then she thought she could actually cope with the fall if she somehow survived. However, Nyssa had no desire to see what awaited her in that black mist.

Nyssa got her wish.

Before she could refocus her vision from the switch, pure white mist enshrouded her. Nyssa could still feel herself falling, but now it felt more like sinking in water. She moved much slower and she could finally catch her breath. She could not see anything though. Nyssa had a strong feeling that the Forgotten Evil did not exist in whatever time this was. At least, it did not exist here.

Nyssa still hit the bottom hard. Luckily, the ground felt as soft as a giant bed sheet. She rolled down at an angle, much further than any bed she had ever seen. She slipped off the sheet and plopped onto a wooden deck. As she gathered her senses, Nyssa realized she was on a boat. The main sail broke her fall and then she rolled off onto the deck. She suspected if the white mist had not slowed her descent, she would have ripped right through the sail and crumpled in a pile of broken timbers.

Those lifesaving mists did not hang all the way to the ground. The hovering fog partially obscured her view, but Nyssa could see much better than expected. She surveyed her surroundings. She thought she stood on what once was a pirate ship. Now all that remained was the deck and a section of railing. The sail hung limp without a breeze.

A short distance away, Nyssa could make out another part of the ship. She thought it was called the prow, but she called it the front. It looked far more damaged than her section, with splintered boards and ropes splayed everywhere.

Nyssa climbed up the sloped deck of her section and grabbed the solid rail for balance. This place looked like a graveyard of long lost things. She spotted a carriage, but no horses to pull it. Nyssa thought it actually resembled an enormous pumpkin. She saw weapons of all types; swords, daggers, hammers, bows and even some she could not identify. She saw a hand mirror, a mangled bird cage, a walking staff and a dented metal lamp which she fully expected to house a genie.

It made Nyssa thankful that she did not see any other people or animals, no bodies and no bones. However, more than any other odd thing, she saw boxes. The boxes came in all shapes and sizes. Most she could hold if she wanted to, but some looked too big and too heavy. Some ornate, some plain. Some looked like treasure chests, while others looked like suitcases. With no exception, every single one had a lock.

Nyssa wanted badly to know what was locked in all these forgotten boxes. Only her desire to now find a way out of the canyon outweighed her curiosity. It appeared that the closest wall was right behind the prow of the ship, a short distance away. Nyssa decided to go that way since she could not see any other walls. The canyon seemed much wider down here and she did not want to switch again while wandering in the mist.

She climbed down from the boat and landed in mud. She had not previously noticed the thick, black mud that covered the floor of the canyon. With each step, Nyssa could hear the mud sucking at her tennis shoes. She soon realized that was the only sound she could hear besides her own breathing. The low hanging mist muffled everything else.

As she got close to the rock wall, Nyssa found it to be completely smooth. She knew she had no chance of climbing, without admitting it would be an impossible climb in any case. Nyssa kicked a small box out of frustration. To her surprise, the lid popped open. Inside, Nyssa saw something that scared her almost as much as the Forgotten Evil.

The cloth lined box had four indentions, perfectly shaped to hold four crystals. Nyssa remembered giving three of these crystals to the elves. She could not imagine what the elves did with them, who could have gathered all four or what they were doing down here. Nyssa knelt on a dry board and reached for one of the crystals. Despite their possible danger, she wanted to make certain they were the same ones.

"Don't touch that," said a voice.

Nyssa yanked her hand back and looked around for whoever scolded her. She saw no one as far as the fog would allow her to see.

"Those are mine. Leave them alone," came the voice again.

This time, Nyssa could tell it was a girl's voice. She did not imagine it. The fog dampened the sound, but it came from somewhere close. Nyssa slowly turned and looked up at the ship.

A girl hung upside down, tangled in ropes, suspended from the prow of the ship. At first, Nyssa thought it was Zandria. She knew it could not be, however, because this girl had striking red hair. It must have been the look in her eyes that made her seem like Zandria, Nyssa decided. The girl looked ready for a fight.

"Get me down from here," she demanded.

The idea of the helpless girl making demands made Nyssa laugh. "Why should I?"

The girl did not answer directly. She said, "I need that case. It's important."

Looking at the crystals, Nyssa knew she wanted nothing to do with them. She wondered for a moment what purpose this girl might have for them, but she did not get a bad feeling. She had an idea to benefit them both.

"Show me the way out," Nyssa said.

"What?" replied the girl.

"Show me how to get out of here and I will help you get down," Nyssa explained.

The girl looked like she was trying to decide. Nyssa felt like neither of them had any other choices.

"Fine," said the girl. "There's a hidden stairway over by the obelisk." She pointed behind Nyssa into the mist.

"Thanks. Now let me find a knife," said Nyssa. With so many things strewn about, she guessed one had to be close. Nyssa found a short curved blade with jagged teeth sticking out of the ground. She pulled it free and climbed the broken ship railing like a ladder. "This will only take a minute."

Nyssa sawed at the ropes and the girl began swaying back and forth uncontrollably. Then Nyssa's vision began to blur. *Not now*, she pleaded in her head. An instant before she switched, she furiously cut through the last thread of the rope. Nyssa believed she saw the girl fall free. Then Nyssa herself fell to the ground.

In whatever time she switched to, the boat had not made its way to the bottom of the canyon. Nyssa hoped the girl's obelisk would still be there, but at least she was not in the belly of the Forgotten Evil right now. She still found plenty of other cases and peculiar objects. Someone had been discarding, *or hiding*, things down here for a long time.

Thankfully, Nyssa found the obelisk poking out of the ground. She expected it to be taller than her like in mummy movies, not the other way around. It must be buried pretty deep, she guessed. Nyssa searched for the hidden stairs along this side of the canyon wall, but found only a few small outcroppings. Nyssa felt trapped, like the girl might have tricked her for her own freedom.

Then something awful and exciting occurred to her.

Nyssa looked at the first stone sticking out at about knee height. She found the next one to her left and almost at her waist. When she spotted the third one near chest height, she had a swirling mix of satisfaction and dread. She knew she found the hidden stairway, but it was not really a stair *way*. She followed the narrow stone steps with her eyes as far as she could. Nyssa had to get out of this before she switched back to the Forgotten Evil. She took the first step. Hugging the wall, she slowly began to scoot upward. She found each outcropping to be only big enough for one foot at a time.

Going through the mist proved to be somewhat difficult. Nyssa took extra care with each step, not wanting to miss in the limited visibility. She had no clue how high she had gone, but did not want to find out by falling. Once she cleared the white fog, her stomach churned. At the same moment she realized how high she was, she also saw how far she still had to go.

After what felt like hours, Nyssa thought she made it to the top. Instead, she discovered a wide ledge sticking out from the canyon wall.

"This is all that holds up the castle?" Nyssa said to no one. It looked like the crystal tower grew out of the wall, toward the middle of the canyon and straight up into the dark, cloudy sky.

She had no desire to risk going back into the castle, so Nyssa searched for the next part of her stairs. Suddenly, flaming chunks of wood crashed behind her. She strained her eyes upward to see a wide gap between the canyon edge and the castle. She guessed that this burning wood was only recently a bridge. Then she thought she saw two horses leap the gap. They were too far away to call for help and quickly disappeared out of sight.

Nyssa continued her climb, now with the added worry of something else falling on her.

Chapter 27

The First Enchantment

The top could not come soon enough. Nyssa could clearly see the ledge, contrasted with the stormy sky. She wanted to hurry, but one wrong step would be the end.

The next moment would always remain in Nyssa's memory.

She switched for the final time.

It came on like every other switch with the blurred vision. Then Nyssa thought she saw light glowing out of her fingertips. She pressed herself flat against the wall in case she lost her balance and squeezed her eyes shut. Her head hurt. Her stomach hurt. Her whole body burned. It took all of her strength to stay on the small steps.

Suddenly, a blast of energy radiated from her body. It knocked her from the outcropping and she started to fall. When Nyssa felt a firm hand around her wrist, she opened her eyes. The blonde haired elf hung over the edge to catch her at the last second. Nyssa saw the other twin directly behind the first and now realized how close to the top she made it on her own.

The elves pulled her up to safety.

Malika said, "I saw you coming up right before you arrived in this time. Fortunately, this is the last safe area. We are being overrun."

The new chaos closed in on Nyssa. She had been alone and quiet for so long that the sound of battle hurt her ears. The Carcharodans seemed much too close.

"They can't win," cried Nyssa. "Not after everything I've been through. Not after everything I've lost." She felt selfish saying it aloud, but she remembered everything. She remembered Kisa, Remina, William, Gulfaxi, Odin, Zandria, Olena and Aleria. She missed Aleria more than anyone she lost in her life. But it was not only her loss. She saw too many lose too much. All of Empyrean was at stake and she blamed herself. She almost wished she could go back to her old life, to being alone. She once tricked herself into thinking her solitude was safe. Then she found Aleria and knew that life was better when it was shared. Nyssa swore that she would not lose this battle if only for Aleria, wherever and whenever she might be.

Nyssa also remembered her lonely nightingale. She looked to the sky, hoping to see him coming to her. She wanted to hear the click of his metallic wings and whir of his beautiful song. Instead of the nightingale, she saw three giant hawks coming toward them. They were not flying wildly like the other birds engaged in the fight. These hawks flew with purpose, each carrying someone on its back.

The hawks landed inside the elves' defensive circle. Three maidens, each of different look and age, dismounted. A small man accompanied one of the girls.

Nyssa examined the new arrivals. One girl dressed in brown leather with a forest green cape. Two blonde braids hung over her shoulders. The fair-skinned one with brown hair looked older, close to eighteen and she wore a beautiful chiffon gown. The little girl could not have been more than five or six. She had dark skin and dark black hair. She looked the most fragile of all of them, but also the most excited by the battle.

The oldest girl introduced herself to Nyssa and the twins, "I am Elyzabel. I believe we have been called."

Nyssa automatically said her name. She believed it was important that they all knew each other as fast as possible.

"They call me Shai," said the youngest girl. "What's going on here?"

"Clearly it's a battle," said the braided girl. She pulled an exquisite axe from behind her back.

"This is Brynn Gunn of the North Woods," said the small man with a gruff voice. "I am her protector, Lowgun."

Nyssa now realized he was a dwarf, like in so many childhood stories. Before she could say anything about it, Malika stepped into the center of the group. She said, "It is time. You four have been called to end the First War for Empyrean. You each have a gift that represents your home. Stand at the four points; North, South, East and West. Deliver your gifts and we will see you do so unharmed."

"I don't quite understand," said Elyzabel.

"Understand that you must go now," answered Malika.

Two elves grabbed Elyzabel and rushed into the fray.

"I get it," said Shai. She clasped her hands together and pressed them to her forehead. She used magic to lift up into the air and float over the Carcharodans heads to the south.

Lowgun turned to Brynn and said, "It looks like I need to clear a path."

They charged to the north side of the canyon, swinging their weapons side to side like clearing a field. Brynn's special axe looked to easily slice through shields and armor.

Nyssa stood alone again at the eastern edge of the canyon. Malika and Marika Lantisphere fought valiantly to keep any enemies from touching her.

She did not notice it previously, but on the opposite side of the canyon, she saw Elyzabel wielding a sword that appeared to be made from that unsettling black rock. Maybe because of their young age, unique weapons or special abilities, Nyssa felt a connection to these strangers.

Oddly, Nyssa could hear each of these girls as if they were still standing next to her. Shai said, "Do you need some help?"

Nyssa could not tell who Shai spoke to, but then Odin burst up from a crowd of Carcharodans. The four evil lieutenants closed in on him immediately.

"We need to get rid of those guys," Shai said playfully. Then she said some kind of magic word, "Tawakafa."

The four powerful lieutenants froze in their tracks. Their arms and legs inexplicably slapped to their bodies as if they had been bound by some invisible rope. Nyssa felt Shai had some powerful magic unlike anything she already experienced in Empyrean.

"Thanks for the compliment, Nyssa," said Shai, as if she read her mind, "but I couldn't have done it on my own."

Nyssa felt their connection strengthen with those words.

"I know right where to put these meanies," said Shai.

The four oily, black giants soared into the air. Then like flaming meteors, Shai dashed them southward, out of sight. Nyssa understood from Shai's thoughts that the lieutenants would be sealed away in a special prison.

"Now. Turn your attention to the pit," instructed Malika.

To her left, Nyssa watched Shai approach the southern edge. She stuck out her hands, with her palms facing the sky. Dark clouds rushed up from the south and spiraled over her. Shai closed her eyes as she whispered a magic spell. The clouds gushed with rain. Before a single drop hit the ground, Shai turned her hands to face each other. All of the rain funneled down into a ball in the space between her hands. The rain kept falling into that ball, but it never grew any bigger.

Shai said, "I have become the Queen of the Southern Valley. I bring my precious drop of water, from which all things live."

Shai's head lolled back and her ball of water exploded like a fountain straight out, flowing directly to the center of the canyon.

Elyzabel stepped to the western edge. She pointed her sword to the sky. Unbelievably, Nyssa could see her clearly across the chasm. She could even see the reflective silver specks in her black sword. Nyssa began to feel warm as Elyzabel spoke, like the words wrapped her in a comfortable blanket.

"I have become the Queen of the Western Sun. I bring my righteous flame, from which all evil is purged," said Elyzabel. She lowered her sword to point it at the center of the pit. Her head tipped back like Shai's. Nyssa thought they might be in some kind of trance now. Then flames shot from the tip of the sword. Like another fountain, the trail of fire burned over the canyon. The searing tongues of flame mingled with the water, not to be extinguished.

Nyssa felt a thousand butterflies take wing in her stomach. She was not ready for it to be her turn. She did not even know what to say.

Brynn said, "My turn."

She turned to Lowgun and jabbed her hand into his beard to retrieve something.

"Hey!" he said.

When she turned back to the canyon, she opened her fist over the northern edge to reveal a handful of dirt. "I have become the Queen of the Northern Wood. I bring my fertile soil, from which all things grow."

She threw the dirt into the air and began spinning her axe by the handle like a powerful fan. As Brynn's head fell back, the dirt rushed out over the canyon in a continuous avalanche.

That left Nyssa.

She felt connected to these girls. They called themselves queens, but Nyssa never felt like a queen, not even a princess. She never wanted the responsibility. She never wanted the attention. She never felt the love.

Looking down into the canyon, Nyssa could see the Forgotten Evil clawing its way out. The black smoke rose with it, enshrouding it. Lightning flashed inside the putrid cloud.

Nyssa missed the feeling of real love until she ran through the door of that strange little shop. In Empyrean, life stopped being only about her. She realized she had to do this for everyone else. She did not need it for herself. She had to become a queen for Aleria and for Empyrean. Then Nyssa remembered the words Olena told her. Afterwards, she could not explain why when they sounded so similar to the other queens that she could not remember them until it came time to speak.

With new found confidence, Nyssa said, "I have become the Queen of the Eastern Sky."

The ground shook and fighting immediately stopped across the battlefield.

"I bring my breath..." started Nyssa. She stopped, wondering what breath she had. She felt like she had nothing to offer. Was she supposed to blow air at the evil monster climbing out of the ground?

But Nyssa had something.

Like everyone told her over and over since coming to Empyrean, she had to trust her abilities. Zandria told her to have confidence in herself. She had something alright.

She finished, "I bring my breath, from which all things start anew."

Nyssa sang a single note. She used her breath to create music. She almost thought for a moment that she could see the music dancing with the earth, fire and water. Then the trance overtook her as well.

Nyssa had a vague recollection of a powerful white light engulfing her body. Odin told her later that the light shone from each of the new queens until it replaced their elements. The shaft of light grew to fill the canyon, burrowing into its depths and striking through the clouds high in the sky. "For a brief moment," Odin said, "it felt like all of Empyrean was bathed in your light."

When Nyssa could open her eyes, things seemed quite different. She felt a warmth and certainty in her heart. And she certainly no longer felt alone. Looking below, she saw that the rising evil had vanished. The threatening black clouds at the bottom settled into a calm white mist. Where their elements had joined over the middle of the pit, now hung a solitary crystal, four powers fused into one.

Even still with superior numbers, the Carcharodans began to retreat. The four lieutenants had been sealed away. The battle was finished.

The Forgotten Evil had been defeated.

Chapter 28

The First Castle

With the last of the Carcharodans gone, the elves began to gather in small camps near the canyon. Odin, Gulfaxi and the Prismata joined the new queens at the Lantisphere camp.

Everyone enjoyed a wondrous show as the newly formed crystal emitted a magnificent light display into the night. Nyssa watched her new friends' faces glow with every color. She busied herself with looking at these strange and amazing people and did not see the crystal change at first. It slowly dropped down into the canyon until it anchored to the wall. Then, like an enchanted seed, it began to grow.

By the time Nyssa looked back, the tower was already far overhead. When it stopped its rapid growth, she guessed it had to be close to one hundred stories tall. She knew it would continue to grow over time as she had personally seen it twice as high.

Frigent Algis and Rontogu Ichikoteru came to speak with Malika and Marika. Nyssa did not hear all of the conversation, but she understood the clans were leaving. Most of them wanted to leave Empyrean entirely. The Rontogu Clan intended to cross the sea, while the Algis Clan planned to explore the ice caps of the far north. Other clans wanted to go south and west.

Malika said, "The Lantispheres will stay in Empyrean. We will find a place in the Northern Wood. It will take some time for all to heal. Humans have a way of attracting trouble and we will distance ourselves from that for some time."

Then Odin offered a few words. He said, "First, I want to honor the Prismata. These sisters helped us greatly and for no cause other than to do good. Sisters, sleep tonight and in the morning, greet us with your colors across the sky. You will shine overhead everyday as a reminder of our promise to keep Empyrean safe from evil."

"It is our honor," said Ruby.

Odin turned to Malika. He said, "Elves, I have made a promise to you as well. With the gift of my life, yours shall be long on this land. A year will be but a day to you."

The twin sisters and the other family heads bowed to Odin. He returned the bows with a smile.

"I, too, will depart from Empyrean," continued Odin. "My power is fading here, but I shall return once a year. On this day, we will celebrate our victory here.

Recalling her time in Banookanook, Nyssa suggested, "We can call it Queen's Day."

"That is a splendid name. It will be a grand holiday," said Odin.

Finally, Odin addressed the four new queens. He said, "Gather you maidens here in times of need or times of peace. The Atumval has left some Deep magic here to keep the Forgotten Evil trapped. This Castle of Empyrean will be the lock on that door until and if the Atumval is ever found. I have already seen the Deep Magic at work in you four. Your powers will grow and always be strongest when you are together."

The four girls held hands. Nyssa truly felt like she finally belonged someplace. Even though she missed Aleria with all of her heart, she felt like she had a family.

"Now, go back to your homelands," said Odin. "The mighty hawks will make their aerie in the tallest spires of this crystal castle. From there, they will spread word of your deed to all of Empyrean. In the north, south, west and east, each build a castle befitting a queen. You will preside over each of these queendoms with fairness, goodness and peace."

The idea seemed to excite Shai the most. She began rambling about everything she would have in her castle. She looked like a happy child with a new toy.

In the morning, a vibrant rainbow filled the sky. Nyssa knew the Prismata would watch over them until the sisters came back to Empyrean. She saw most of the elves left during the night. She could find no sign of Father Odin or the mighty Gulfaxi.

The young queens said their farewells and each left for their own homeland.

Chapter 29

The First Journey Comes to an End

One hundred years passed.

Nyssa grew to be a kind and loving queen. She remembered almost nothing of her life before Empyrean, but she never forgot Aleria.

Her castle, Soria Moria, stood tall and proud. The doors remained open for anyone under the Eastern Sky. Villages like Bremen and Fountainhead began to spring up throughout the beautiful forests.

On the first anniversary of Queen's Day, Father Odin came to visit Nyssa. Before he left, he promised, "I shall always remember you."

After that day, she never saw him again. Still, every child under her reign never missed a present from Father Odin on Queen's Day.

As Nyssa instructed, her gatekeeper never turned anybody away from Soria Moria. She met with countless people to share stories and ideas. She especially loved meeting musicians. Nyssa held great parties where they would sing late into the night.

Then one day, a stranger came to her.

The man, with a slightly balding head and wire frame glasses hanging on his nose, seemed familiar. Maybe he had been to Soria Moria before, thought Nyssa. She could not recall his name and none of her courtiers seemed to recognize him.

"May I have your name?" asked the now gray haired queen.

"I apologize," said the peculiar man. "It is the only one I have, so I prefer not to give it away."

This amused Nyssa enough to listen to what the stranger had to say. He presented her with a thick, leather bound book. She opened it, only to find hundreds of blank pages.

"What kind of story is this?" asked Nyssa.

"The best kind," said the man. "The one you write for yourself."

The queen replied, "What shall I write then?"

"Everything," he said simply. "Put everything in it since you first set foot in Empyrean. Write about it all up to this very moment. Don't leave anything out, not even the bit you were told to leave out by those spectacular sisters."

Nyssa wondered how he could possibly know about her meeting with Zandria and Olena. She never told anyone. Nyssa studied this odd man's face. He knew things and apparently he felt it was important for her to write her story. She could not shake the feeling that she knew him once, maybe long ago.

She said, "Karl?"

"Hmm?" he answered with a raised eyebrow. His reaction did not confirm or deny her suspicion. She thought she met him once, briefly in those crazy time-switching days when she first came to Empyrean, but could not say for certain. And he was no help clarifying any of it.

Before he left, he finished with some instructions, "Your journal will be important for the queens who come after you."

"Like Remina and Olena," said Nyssa.

He said, "Don't forget Aurora and Minerva come before them."

Left alone with the empty book, Nyssa spent many days trying to fill its pages. She remembered everything and told it in the order that it happened to her. She tried to put in references to let others know the different times she visited, but she did not know all of them herself. She found the most difficult writing to be when she lost Aleria. That special girl never left her heart.

Nyssa decided to end her story with a song.

When I was but a child, I danced upon the shore
But I grew older, wiser and the dancing came no more.
In a land of make believe, I found my one true friend
As time moved on and I grew up our adventures had to end.

The stories tell of elves and queens
Of dinosaurs and wicked beings,
The path I walked along with you
To do the deed I had to do

I am happier now than I was back then
When I lost my only friend.
This song I write is for you,
My feelings here are always true.

When I was a queen upon a throne, I listened with my heart.
But I was a child once before, knowing nothing from the start.
In a land of make believe, I had to find my way.
This is my home, this is my life, forever will I stay.

A frozen prince and unicorns,
Rainbows in the morn.
Four maidens came from afar
Gathered now, queens they are

I am happier now then I was back then
Until I found my only friend.
This song I write is for me
That in my heart you'll always be.

Chapter 30

The First Tale is Told

Tym closed the ancient book. He said, "Now you know the story of the First Queen."

Olena looked around the pale, candle lit room. Kez had fallen asleep. Dew seemed lost in thought, maybe thinking about her ancestors. Tears streamed down Eisenhahn's face. This made Olena want to cry too.

"Why are you crying?" she asked the metal man.

"I miss Aleria," he said between sobs.

"Me too," said Olena.

Zandria tried to console him. "Maybe we can look for her some day?"

"I'd like that," said Eisenhahn.

Adam jumped up from the table. Eisenhahn reached for the boy's half eaten cake. "Doesn't anybody have a problem with this?" said Adam.

"What do you mean?" asked Tym.

Olena thought Adam looked angry. He said, "I'm pretty sure that book told us that Zandria and Olena met Nyssa."

"We did," volunteered Olena, "on our way to get cake."

"You didn't think to tell us?" asked Adam, looking directly at Zandria.

"I was going to tell you after the story. I'm sorry," said Zandria. "We can talk about it more tomorrow. There's plenty in that story to talk about."

Everybody started to leave the room, ready for bed. Olena made her way to Tym and tugged on his tunic.

She said, "You forgot to say one thing."

"What is that, Your Majesty?" Tym asked.

Olena said, "The End."

About this book

Is it true you can never go home?

As a foster child, Nyssa longed for a home. When she stepped through the door of a curious little oddity shop, she was about to learn a new meaning of the word home. She enters the fairy tale world of Empyrean only to find she's come unraveled and bounces through the history of that fantasy land. The girl discovers a world both frightening and exciting. She makes new friends and terrible enemies.

After walking through that door, Nyssa lands in the middle of an epic battle of good versus evil. The Forgotten Evil is poised to escape as Nyssa struggles with her own coming of age in a race to save Empyrean.

Lost in time with time running out, Nyssa has to choose between duty and friendship.

What would you chose?

This time travel adventure is the fourth book of the young adult fantasy series The Empyrical Tales.

About the author

As a best-selling author and publisher, Mark has won various awards for writing and book cover design.

Growing up in Kansas, Mark graduated from Sumner Academy of the Arts and Sciences and received his Bachelor's in Film from the University of Kansas.

Mark has written under a few pen names with numerous novels, screenplays, short stories and digital series to his credit.